"I'm editor-in-chief and president of the school newspaper, as well as Tsukuyomi Magic Academy's idol, Ivy!"

Ivy

Head of the *Tsukuyomi Academy Newspaper*. A rabbitfolk girl who's always fired up. Knows the roles the Three Committees play.

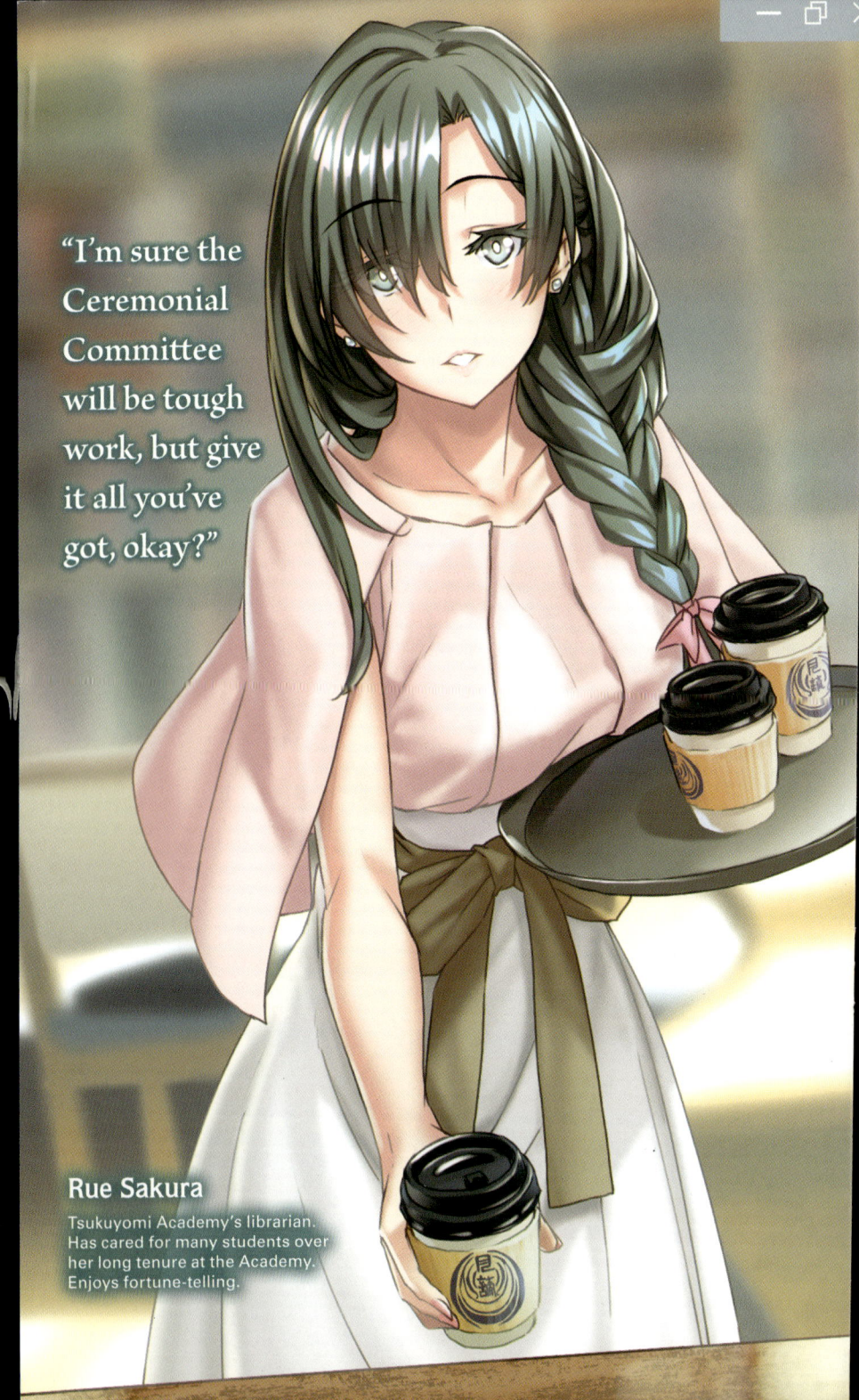

Magical★Explorer
Volume 4
Reborn as a Side Character in a Fantasy Dating Sim

Iris

ILLUSTRATION BY
Noboru Kannatuki

New York

Magical★Explorer: Reborn as a Side Character in a Fantasy Dating Sim, Vol. 4

Iris

Translation by David Musto
Cover art by Noboru Kannatuki

This book is a work of fiction. Names, characters, places, and incidents are the product of the author's imagination or are used fictitiously. Any resemblance to actual events, locales, or persons, living or dead, is coincidental.

MAGICAL★EXPLORER ERO GAME NO YUJIN KYARA NI TENSEI SHITAKEDO, GAME CHISHIKI TSUKATTE JIYUNI IKIRU Vol. 4
©Iris, Noboru Kannatuki 2021
First published in Japan in 2021 by KADOKAWA CORPORATION, Tokyo.
English translation rights arranged with KADOKAWA CORPORATION, Tokyo through TUTTLE-MORI AGENCY, INC., Tokyo.

English translation © 2023 by Yen Press, LLC

Yen Press, LLC supports the right to free expression and the value of copyright. The purpose of copyright is to encourage writers and artists to produce the creative works that enrich our culture.

The scanning, uploading, and distribution of this book without permission is a theft of the author's intellectual property. If you would like permission to use material from the book (other than for review purposes), please contact the publisher. Thank you for your support of the author's rights.

Yen On
150 West 30th Street, 19th Floor
New York, NY 10001

Visit us at yenpress.com ★ facebook.com/yenpress ★ twitter.com/yenpress ★ yenpress.tumblr.com ★ instagram.com/yenpress

First Yen On Edition: March 2023
Edited by Yen On Editorial: Maya Deutsch
Designed by Yen Press Design: Andy Swist

Yen On is an imprint of Yen Press, LLC.
The Yen On name and logo are trademarks of Yen Press, LLC.

The publisher is not responsible for websites (or their content) that are not owned by the publisher.

Library of Congress Cataloging-in-Publication Data
Names: Iris (Light novel author), author. | Kannatuki, Noboru, illustrator. | Musto, David, translator.
Title: Magical explorer / Iris ; illustration by Noboru Kannatuki ; translation by David Musto.
Other titles: Magical explorer. English
Description: First Yen On edition. | New York, NY : Yen On, 2021–
Identifiers: LCCN 2021039072 | ISBN 9781975325619 (v. 1 ; trade paperback) | ISBN 9781975325633 (v. 2 ; trade paperback) | ISBN 9781975325657 (v. 3 ; trade paperback) | ISBN 9781975350482 (v. 4 ; trade paperback)
Subjects: CYAC: Video games—Fiction. | Role playing—Fiction. | Magic—Fiction. | Fantasy. | LCGFT: Light novels.
Classification: LCC PZ7.1.I76 Mag 2021 | DDC [Fic]—dc23
LC record available at https://lccn.loc.gov/2021039072

ISBNs: 978-1-9753-5048-2 (paperback)
978-1-9753-5049-9 (ebook)

10 9 8 7 6 5 4 3 2 1

LSC-C

Printed in the United States of America

Chapter Select

Magical★Explorer

CONTENTS

▶ » Chapter 1　　001 **Daily Life**	▶ » Chapter 2　　007 **Seeds of Possibility**
▶ » Chapter 3　　033 **The Three Committees**	▶ » Chapter 4　　049 **Us from Here on Out**
▶ » Chapter 5　　065 **Bienvenue, Ceremonial Committee**	▶ » Chapter 6　　079 **A Dangerous Machine**
▶ » Chapter 7　　087 **The Hijiri Siblings**	▶ » Chapter 8　　105 **Dungeon: Archives of Promise**
▶ » Chapter 9　　125 **Yuika Hijiri**	▶ » Chapter 10　　141 **Her Name Was Gabby, Gabriella Evangelista**
▶ » Chapter 11　　153 **Mystery**	▶ » Chapter 12　　157 **Thus Was the Eroge Protagonist**
▶ » ——　　165 **Afterword**	

Illustration: Noboru Kannatuki
Graphic Design: Kai Sugiyama (Tsuyoshi Kusano Design Co., Ltd.)

Characters

Magical★Explorer 3

Kousuke Takioto

The best friend character from *Magical★Explorer*. The soul of a Japanese eroge afficionado dwells within him. Possesses a unique ability.

Ludie

Ludivine Marie-Ange de la Tréfle.

Highborn second daughter to the emperor of the elven Tréfle Empire. A main heroine who appears on the game packaging for *Magical★Explorer*.

Nanami

A maid created to assist Dungeon Masters. Belongs to the angel race, who are few in number.

Marino Hanamura

Principal of Tsukuyomi Magic Academy, the game's main setting. Receives limited screen time in the game, so she's shrouded in mystery.

Hatsumi Hanamura

Marino Hanamura's daughter and Kousuke's second cousin. Generally very quiet and reserved. Teaches at Tsukuyomi Magic Academy.

Claris

Elf who serves as Ludie's bodyguard and maid. Serious and devoted to her mistress, she has a tendency to beat herself up over her failures.

Iori Hijiri

The main character in the game version of *Magical★Explorer*. Ordinary in appearance. When developed, however, he becomes the strongest character in the game.

Yuika Hijiri

Iori Hijiri's younger stepsister. A main heroine who is featured on the game's box art. Transferred to Tsukuyomi Magic Academy.

Rina Katou

Katorina.

One of the main heroines present on the *Magical★Explorer* box art. A competitive spirit who is sensitive about her meager bust.

Monica

Monica Mercedes von Mobius.

The president of the Student Council. One of *Magical★Explorer's* Big Three and a main heroine who features on the game's packaging.

Stef

Stefania Scaglione.

Serves as the captain of the Morals Committee. The Acting Saint from Leggenze. Although she is beautiful, compassionate, and popular with the students… is there more to her than meets the eye…?

Benito

Benito Evangelista.

Serves as the ceremonial minister, the president of the Ceremonial Committee. Despised by the students of the Academy, but beloved by eroge players.

Fran

Franziska Edda von Gneisenau.

Serves as Vice President of the Student Council. An extremely earnest and diligent girl. Sees Yukine and Shion as her rivals.

Yukine Mizumori

One of the officially recognized overpowered characters who are collectively referred to as the Big Three of *Magical★Explorer*. Lieutenant of the Morals Committee.

Shion Himemiya

Serves as Ceremonial Vice Minister of the Ceremonial Committee. Always clad in a kimono instead of her uniform. Her strength is on par with the other main heroines'.

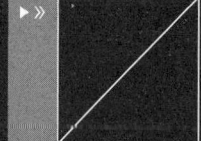

Ms. Ruija

Instructor at Tsukuyomi Magic Academy. Loose with money and indebted to the Hanamura family. Was Hatsumi's senior during their student days and challenged dungeons alongside her.

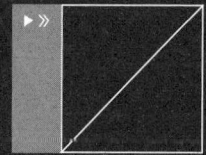

Chapter 1 — Daily Life

Magical★Explorer

Reborn as a Side Character in a Fantasy Dating Sim

Had life ever gone this well for me before?

I didn't know if this was a reaction from my solo dungeon adventure—the experiences it gave me, or the emotions it brought up in me—but the everyday world looked more vibrant and colorful than ever. It wasn't lost on me why things seemed that way; it was because of Ludie, Yukine, Nanami, Sis—because everyone was here with me.

These girls had brightened my world, so I needed to give them... give...them...

Wait a minute.

"I feel it would be much more visible if placed right past the school gate, rather than in the plaza in front of the Academy."

"Good point...!"

"Hold on a second."

"What is it, Master?"

"Kousuke?"

Sis and Nanami both looked very serious, while Ludie seemed exasperated as she gazed my way.

The situation made me kind of uneasy.

I wanted to have a pretty serious conversation with them right now, but there was something I needed to figure out before I could broach the subject.

"What exactly are you doing?"

Sis and Nanami were talking to each other while examining a sheet of paper covered in monetary estimates with far too many zeroes. Sis's expression might've seemed to be the same as always, but I could tell—the look on her face meant she was truly serious.

"Simple! We were thinking of erecting a statue to commemorate the unprecedented record you set."

Ohhh, a statue? That was it? I was relieved—I'd been imagining something far more outrageous.

"What in the world are you going on about, silly? A statue? That'd be super embarrassing. It'd be a waste of money, too. No thank you! ♪"

Obviously, I didn't need an effigy, but it tickled me to think I had been able to accomplish something grand enough to warrant commemoration. All my hard work had paid off.

"I'm overjoyed to see you so smitten with the idea. Why don't we call the statue 'Nanami's Grand Slam'?"

"Wait, it's of *you*?! Not me?!"

Who do you think set that record?! This guy! Why would you put up an effigy of yourself? I could admit that a representation of Nanami would be much more attractive, but I was clearly the one deserving of it.

"Nanami's just joking. It would be of you, Kousuke."

Oh, thank goodness. What a relief. I was clearly the one who should be getting an effigy, right? That being said...

"Really? A statue of me, huh? I'm flattered, but that's definitely unnecessary."

"It's just, while we have gotten permission from the Academy for a commemorative sculpture, the expenditures behind it are a different story..."

Hello? Was anyone listening to me? Though, on second thought—

"If you're being serious, then I'm gonna have to go complain to Marino later."

—how were they actually able to get permission for this?

That woman was a despot working simultaneously as both the principal and the chairwoman of the Academy board. Any approvals had to go through her. So why the heck had she given them the go-ahead to build it?

"She prattled on about how she would approve the construction immediately if you erected an effigy of her next to yours, but it goes without saying it should be I, your loyal and faithful maid, who should get a place at your side. Naturally, she denied *that* proposal."

So that's all Marino would have needed to fund this statue, huh? Yeah, I was going to raise my grievances to her later. For sure.

"Whatever the circumstances, it isn't happening. Who the hell needs a statue?"

Nanami gave a small sigh and shook her head in exasperated resignation.

"...And after all the trouble we went through to plan this out... What a shame. This transgression will cost you five of your Nanami Points."

"Nanami Points? What are those even supposed to be? Ah, whatever. By the way, how many do I have right now?"

"Five hundred sixty million points, I believe."

"Then five's basically just a rounding error!"

Would anyone notice five yen missing from a pile of five hundred sixty million yen? Of course not!

"What a truly wonderfully moving follow-up quip, Master. That's another three thousand points."

"What is with these increments?! I'm just getting more and more..."

"Incidentally, the max number of points is one hundred."

"How many laps have I done around *that* then?!"

"Now you've made me all self-conscious."

"Don't get bashful on me. That wasn't a compliment."

If anything, I should be the one getting complimented for amassing so many points.

"Don't worry, Kousuke."

Worry? That was clearly going to be unnecessary because I had a hunch about what was coming up next.

"You've also cleared the eight hundred million Big Sis Point benchmark, too."

Whew boy, I was in trouble. I didn't have enough comebacks to keep up with them both... What were Big Sis Points, then? And why were they "Big Sis" Points, huh? Hatsumi had referred to herself as "Big Sis" way back when, too—just how much did she want me to call her that? It was embarrassing, but I supposed I could give it a try just once.

"Oh really...? Thanks, Big Sis."

"That's another one billion Big Sis Points!!"

"But that dropped your Nanami Points by fifty thousand."

"Why?!"

"I was kidding about you losing points... *Sigh*."

It definitely didn't *sound* like she was kidding. Ah, whatever.

Putting all that aside... How can I express it? I guess it felt like I had instantly fallen back into everyday life. It felt refreshing to be back to this silly routine after spending a full week in the dungeon.

"All right, back on topic. What do you think, Ludie?"

"Huh?!"

Ludie turned to me in confusion when I brought her into the conversation, her face somewhat flushed; she must not have been paying attention.

"U-um, well, your Ludie Points, that's a bit………you know…"

"Uh, Ludie?"

"Wh-wh-wh-what?!"

"Why're you talking about the points stuff? The statue, I mean the statue!"

"Sheesh, *that's* what you meant," Ludie murmured, slightly lowering her eyes. "A statue seems quite egotistical and overly self-confident, so I can't really condone the idea."

Yup, she was right on the money. What a fantastic way of putting it. Now I needed Ludie to go explain that to the two clowns going over the construction estimate.

"Maybe if it was a chibi doll instead, though…"

"Right, maybe if it was a chibi figure…… Uh, nope, I don't need that either, actually!"

A wonderful idea, but who in the world would want that?! Was Nanami getting to her? Why was she playing the stooge here? I needed her to help me keep up with the other two!

"O-of course! I was just joking!"

"Ah well, whatever. By the way, where's Yukine?"

"She had some Discipline Committee business and headed back with Marino. Said they needed to put a bunch of restrictions in place before any first years go off and do something reckless."

Huh, so they were worried students might get into trouble, eh? Were there any students like that here…? That sounded awfully familiar…

"It's probably your fault, Kousuke."

"Yeah, you're right. I'll go apologize later."

"Yukine didn't seem to really mind too much. She looked like she was enjoying herself, in fact."

While Ludie and I talked, Nanami and Sis once again started conversing among themselves, grave looks on their faces.

▶ Chapter 1: Daily Life

"...So, what are you two whispering about?"

"We've seen the light, to be honest. We've realized we should make chibi dolls instead."

"I want one. They'd sell, too."

"Yeah, right! No one's buying those."

Like there was anyone out there who'd want a chibi doll of me...right? Definitely not. Heck, if anything...

"I feel like it'd be a better idea to make Ludie, Sis, and Nanami figures instead. I'd want them, for sure."

"O-of me?!"

"No more 'Big Sis'...?"

"Why have a chibi version when you have the real deal right here waiting for you?"

My comment had produced three totally different reactions, one of which was wholly incomprehensible.

"A Ludie doll would go flying off the shelves. Especially with those LLL guys."

"Ugh......"

Ludie looked extremely displeased all of a sudden. Now that I thought about it, she really despised LLL.

"Ah yes," Nanami muttered as she fiddled with her Tsukuyomi Traveler. "Those people who cannot understand Master's grandeur. I've considered swapping out their toilet paper for sandpaper."

"Don't you think that's extreme?!"

Their butts would turn into a river of blood!

"You should have done it anyway."

Ludie had no patience left for her fan club.

Nanami abruptly shared the screen of her Tsukuyomi Traveler with Sis, who excitedly jumped up and left the room with her.

"By the way..."

Ludie broke the silence as I watched the other two leave.

"You were talking about points and stuff, right?"

"Yeah, that's right."

She tilted her head down. Her cheeks were tinged red for some reason. Then, using her right hand to play with her hair, she suddenly looked off in the opposite direction and let out a small yet audible gulp.

"Um, well, it's just… If I had any points like that to give, then you'd h-have the most of anyone, Kousuke!"

After saying this, Ludie leapt to her feet.

She then left the room—or at least tried to, slamming her shoulder into the door before finally departing with a look of mortification on her face.

 CONFIG

Chapter 2 — Seeds of Possibility

Magical★Explorer
Reborn as a Side Character in a Fantasy Dating Sim

Marino and Yukine eventually returned home, both in high spirits. I headed straight to Nanami's room once I finished my dinner.

I knocked, and she opened the door.

"Why Master, what are you doing here at such a late hour? Hurry, come inside and warm yourself by the fire."

"Is this supposed to be an alpine hut in the middle of a blizzard or something? T-shirt weather's just around the corner, you know."

"Let's leave the jokes at the door, then. Now, by process of elimination, I'm assuming you must be here to……sneak into my bed for the night and make love?"

"What 'process of elimination' led you to conclude *that*?"

Wouldn't that be the very first option to be eliminated? Well, I supposed that wasn't necessarily the case in eroge.

"Putting that aside, what can I do for you?"

Nanami pulled out a chair for me, so I took a seat.

"Sorry about barging in without notice, but I wanted you to take a look at this."

Saying this, I took out a few seeds. Then I placed them on top of her desk.

One, two, three, four, five. Five gold seeds that I had collected in the Academy dungeon. Nanami looked at them and let out a small sigh.

"…So the reason you were so obstinate about clearing the first forty layers solo in a week…"

"Yeah, it was to get these."

Of course a Maid Knight built to serve a Dungeon Master would know this stuff.

One glance was all it took for Nanami to realize what the seeds were. Not only that, but she picked up on how I had obtained them, too. That being said, the one-week time limit didn't determine whether you could get the seeds or not, but I didn't need to correct her on that.

"That's quite the item you've gotten your hands on, there. Just how many Dungeon Points... Even Dungeon Masters rarely meddle with these things."

"Really?"

"Yes, it's true. I never would have expected you to get any. Impressive as always, Master. However...could you sit down there on your knees for me?" Nanami requested, a big smile spreading across her face. She pointed to a spot on the floor.

I looked where she was gesturing before turning back to her again.

She pulled back her hand before again pointing to the ground with a smile on her face.

"Uhhh, why?"

"Don't worry about it. Just sit on the floor, Master."

I could sense that Nanami was a little peeved, so I quickly sat on the ground with my legs tucked under me.

"Master. I believe you already know this, but these seeds you have here are quiiiiite the rare item. So rare that I'm honestly stunned to see them."

"S-sure."

"I surmise from you mentioning 'solo' and the number of layers, 'forty' exactly, that you knew how to obtain these from the start, yes? No, you definitely knew beforehand, didn't you? Needless to say, I am extremely curious as to how you acquired this information. I won't interrogate you on that point. But."

"But?"

"How could you do something so reckless? That's something I cannot overlook."

There was clearly a smile on Nanami's face, but she wasn't happy at all. Okay, so she was actually grinning, but there was a subtle anger radiating from her whole body.

"I-I don't know, was it really that reckless? I d-didn't really have too much trouble."

I'd figured out why she wanted me to get down on my knees. But trying to smooth things over by downplaying my deeds wasn't proving very fruitful.

▶ Chapter 2: Seeds of Possibility

"Let me give you an example, then. Where does a bank store its deposits?"

"W-well, I mean, I'd imagine in a really firmly secured vault?"

"Dungeons operate under the same logic. Let's suppose that Seeds of Possibility are installed inside a dungeon to raise its value. The thing is, the Dungeon Master doesn't want anyone to take them, either. In that case, how do you think they would implement them?"

So dungeons could be more or less valuable, huh...? Prying any further was likely to kick up a hornet's nest or involve asking Nanami something she couldn't readily answer, so I decided to drop the topic there.

"U-uh, let's see, they'd tighten up security?"

"Exactly. I went ahead and did some research into the Tsukuyomi Academy Dungeon. To be perfectly honest, I actually thought the thirtieth layer would be just about perfect for you before you started to feel the pinch. Nevertheless."

"Nevertheless?"

"Knowing you and your abilities, Master, I suspected you would have some sort of trick up your sleeve to clear them all. But."

Nanami glared at me reproachfully.

"It couldn't have been trivial."

In truth, everything Nanami had said was right on the mark. I'd been able to weaken Icarus and put myself into a mysterious trance to overcome him, but he normally appeared much deeper down in the dungeon, around the eightieth layer. I'd only managed to finish him off by exploiting his vulnerability to fire.

"Do you understand? Without some veeeeery, and I do mean veeeery extraordinary luck, you shouldn't have been able to obtain these. I take it you must have dealt with some difficult maze-style floors, trap-filled floors, or a high-level boss, correct? There definitely had to be *something* like that down there."

"......"

Everything Nanami had described was so spot-on that I was at a loss for words.

"Why didn't you turn back around? You only get one body, Master, and you need to take care of it... If you still wish to go off somewhere dangerous, then bring me with you at the very least... Please, Master."

Her plea practically pierced right through me. Of all the countless words I had exchanged with Nanami up until now, these hit me the hardest.

"...Sorry. I'll be careful."

Hearing this, Nanami relaxed her face and smiled with a chuckle.

"I really am begging you... Honestly, if you really had died on me, you'd be sending a stray maid out into the cold, you know. Keep that in mind."

"What the hell's a 'stray maid'?" I said with a strained grin.

For a moment, I considered telling her to go work for someone else instead, but stopped myself at the last second. I couldn't say that to her. While I remained silent, Nanami sat me down on the sofa and bowed.

"Well, um, as long as you understand what I mean, that's enough. Also, allow me to apologize, Master. My comments went too far... I am sure I must have offended you. Please punish me however you see fit."

Nanami's statement brought another strained smile to my face.

"...Why the heck do I need to punish you for making it clear you're worried about me?"

"I am still nothing more than a humble Maid Knight. Normally, I would never be allowed to act like this."

She had forced her master to sit on the floor and all. Not that it bothered me in the slightest.

"All right, I'll give you my permission, then... From here on out, I want you to speak candidly to me."

"...In truth, uttering what I did just now was an act of folly. It could have easily gotten me fired from the company—the worst possible thing that can happen to you as a maid."

"Let's put it this way, then. I'm glad you told me what you did and said you were worried about me. Thank you. Your company might think it's out of line or whatever, but from my perspective, you said the best thing I could've heard, and you're the greatest maid I could ever ask for. I doubt I'll ever run into someone from that company of yours, but if I do, I'll go ahead and tell them the same."

At my words, Nanami squinted slightly, and a gentle, slightly bashful grin spread across her face.

"There you go building up points again, Master. If I were anyone else, that comment would've been really dangerous, you know. That would have induced Heart-Throbbing Eternal Destiny, for sure. But somehow, I managed to get off with completely falling for you instead."

"You still fell in love, though?! And again with the points stuff… How many do I have now, then?"

"Let's see, hmmm, seventy-three billion points."

"Oh, wow, seventy-three billion, huh—wait seventy-three *billion*?! What the hell happened in the past few hours to give me a hundred times as much?!"

"Seeing as you earned one billion points from Hatsumi, I couldn't let her get the better of me, so I made sure to tack on a few ten billion or so myself."

"Seriously…that's all it took to earn them…?"

Nanami brought a hand to her mouth and giggled. Seeing her response, I was coaxed to laugh alongside her.

"But enough about points. This isn't meant to be an apology for worrying you or anything, but I want you to have this." I picked up one of the Seeds of Possibility and offered it to her. Just as I did, her smile disappeared, and she narrowed her eyes.

"What in the world are you doing? How could you give an item that even dungeon masters find valuable enough to safeguard to someone like me? Is your mind addled? Are you self-sabotaging? Just take a moment to compose yourself, please, Master."

She tried pushing my outstretched hand aside as she spoke.

"I'm plenty composed, believe me. I thought things over and over again, but ultimately concluded my first instinct was the right one."

Naturally, I had mulled over how I would use the seeds before I even went into the dungeon.

To be honest, I'd also thought about exchanging them for Tsukuyomi Points and buying up all the items I could ever want. But my desire to have everyone use the seeds for themselves was greater than my lust for items, and my time in the dungeon had only reinforced these convictions.

"I was only able to get this far thanks to you all, and it'll be impossible to move onto the next steps without everyone, too."

I'd always considered strengthening my companions the same as strengthening myself.

There were bound to be many dungeons from here on out that I wouldn't be able to handle solo. Difficult monsters I would need a team to take down, and events I wouldn't stand a ghost of a chance clearing alone.

Nevertheless, those sorts of places were home to the truly worthwhile items and farming locations this world had to offer. Not only that, but there were also areas where I could efficiently grind up a lot of money and experience by fighting with multiple people on my side.

"You said it yourself, Nanami—the Academy Dungeon was actually pretty tough. Made me keenly aware that I'd have a real rough time pushing ahead any more on my own."

This prompted a glare from Nanami. She didn't say a word, but I picked up on what she was implying immediately.

"S-sorry. Anyway, I feel bad about this, Nanami, but I'd like you to lend me your strength from here on out, too. Which is all the more reason why I want you to accept this," I said, holding out the seed to her. She looked at it and shook her head in exasperation.

"What are you talking about, Master? I've said as much to you before. My place is wherever you are."

She stood up and gave a curtsy fit for a maid.

"I'll always be your maid no matter what, and that will hold firm and true whatever lies in store for us," Nanami said before taking one of the seeds in her hand. "If you insist, then I suppose I have little choice otherwise. Now, I believe this means it's time for me to offer up my everything, body and soul, isn't it?"

Whoa, waaaaaaay too heavy.

"Save the silly stuff and just take it, will you…?"

"Fine, then. Have you given these to the others already?"

"No, not yet."

Nanami cocked her head at my reply.

"Just why then……did you come to me first?"

"I figure you're the one I'm going to be consulting with and taking on dungeons with the most from here on out. Now that I think about it, I feel a bit bad, actually. Dragging you around with me like that."

Nanami knew a lot about dungeons and could understand the ancient language used in them, though she probably couldn't reveal too much about their inner workings to me. I was going to have a lot to discuss with her.

Her flawless trap-related skills made her an even more valuable

▶ Chapter 2: Seeds of Possibility

person to go on expeditions with. I was inevitably going to be inviting her to tag along more and more often. Also, Ludie and Yukine were still Academy students at the end of the day, so there was a chance they'd be unable to come help me clear dungeons for one reason or another.

"Really? Well, then I can expect your level of reliance on me to soar to outstanding heights...!"

"I mean, I trust you so much, it's honestly impossible to even quantify."

The same was true for Ludie and Yukine, too.

Nanami widened her eyes and started stuttering, like a goldfish gasping for oxygen.

"...I-I said you were at seventy-three billion points, but in truth, you're actually at a specific but impossible to quantify number, so my trust is eternal and..."

"What're you turning this into a competition for?"

Plus, I didn't have a clue what she was saying.

"Let's put aside the jokes for now. Have you used one of these seeds yourself, Master?"

"Not yet, actually."

"In that case, let us both use them together."

I went to put a seed in my mouth......when Nanami stopped me.

"Were you aware, Master? There is in fact a special way to eat these seeds."

"...Really?"

"Yes, that's right. We need to feed each other: Master feeding his maid, and maid feeding her Mas—that's quite a suspicious look you're giving me."

"That's obviously not true."

"If you stick with something long enough, it can eventually become fact."

"That's just outright admitting you were lying, isn't it?"

When I swallowed the seed in my hand, Nanami placed hers in her mouth. Then my body......didn't undergo any changes.

"Don't worry, I assure you that the effects will manifest soon. Anyway, what will you do with the rest of these seeds?"

"Right, so you, me, Ludie, and Yukine are a given... After that, I thought I'd give one to either Sis or Claris."

"I see... A reasonable approach."

"It's bothering me a bit that I'll have to choose between Claris and Sis. Oh, and that I won't be able to give one to Marino, either..."

"Rest assured, Marino Hanamura is the last person who would need one of these. I'll go settle things with her, so please handle Ludie and the others, Master."

It always struck me how Marino was the one person Nanami displayed open hostility to.

"Got it. Then I guess I'll go to everyone else's rooms after this."

"If you're slipping in for a steamy nighttime rendezvous, be sure to include me in the mix."

"I won't be! And spare me the cryptic nonsense."

Oh how I longed to ask what exactly was the point of having *both* of us there for such a visit.

I took a sidelong glance at Nanami, who seemed to be plotting something, and asked her about something that had suddenly drawn my attention.

"Oh, right. By the way..."

"What is it?"

"Those papers on your desk have got me curious. What are they supposed to be?" I said, turning my gaze toward the bundle.

"Oh, those all have to do with the figure......"

"Figure...?"

"...figures that Miss Ruija still owes. I was thinking up plans on how to resolve the situation."

"Now that's a difficult problem, huh."

Aiming for perfect marks on my tests at school would've been an easier goal.

"Sure, but is that really it? I feel like I saw the word 'chibi' on there... and something about sizes..."

"Well, it's important to strike while the iron's hot, yes, Master? Please go give everyone your seed...uh, *these* seeds."

"Hey, wait..."

Nanami pushed me out the door.

I headed straight for Marino's room and knocked on the door.

"Oh, what is it, Kousuke? Come for a steamy nighttime rendezvous?"

"You know, I wonder about how everyone in this house lost their minds."

The likelier explanation was that Nanami and Marino were simply both eccentrics. Though Sis qualified for the moniker as well, in some respects.

"Only kidding, of course. What's the matter?"

Nanami said she would come settle things with Marino later, but this was obviously something she should hear from me directly. Especially if I didn't end up giving her one of the seeds after all.

"Oh my," Marino immediately gasped when I produced the three remaining Seeds of Possibility in front of her.

"Wooow, you've got something special, there."

"Yes, I certainly do."

Marino's smile didn't break as she stared at the seeds in my hands. Despite the fact that she understood exactly what they were, she still didn't seem shaken in the slightest.

"You're not surprised, even knowing what these are?"

"Of all my predictions for you, this was definitely on the more outlandish end of the spectrum. I may not show it, but I'm *very* surprised, you know. I don't even feel like teasing you right now."

"...You don't seem shocked to me."

"Oh no, I'm definitely surprised. I'm surprised in a number of ways, actually."

"In a number of ways...?"

"Yep, a whole bunch. I honestly want to go into detail about all sorts of things right now, but unfortunately, that's not at my discretion."

In other words, she had no plans to answer my questions.

"So? You wanted to talk to me about something, right?"

I nodded slightly.

"I'm unsure about who I should give these to."

"Hmmm, just to be clear, you've already used one yourself, right?"

"I did. Both on myself and Nanami."

"Really...?"

It was then that I finally saw a look of genuine shock on Marino's face.

"On good old Nanami, did you...? So what're you going to do with the rest, then?"

Nanami definitely would've gotten mad at Marino for calling her that.

"That's what I wanted to talk to you about. I was thinking of handing them out to everyone."

"Hmmm, you've got three here."

"Yup. These are all I've got."

Marino suddenly narrowed her eyes.

"Let me ask you what you're thinking here, then. The truth is, you've pretty much decided who you're going to give these to already, haven't you?"

"Well, I did think it through to some extent already, but...wow, you really saw this coming. That I had already thought it through myself, I mean."

"Well, Kou dear, you always end up mulling these things over before you come asking for advice, right?"

I mean, I thought it was reasonable to come to my own conclusions before asking other people for their opinions on something. But that was neither here nor there.

"Anyway, as for who I'm giving these to..."

"Go on."

"Ludie and Yukine are both getting a seed for sure. The last one would either go to Claris or Sis. I was thinking I'd give you and whoever's left a seed after I get more of them."

I got that far when Marino put her hand up to her cheeks and gave me an exasperated glare.

"Hold on... You plan on getting more of these?"

"Yes, exactly."

There were various paths to acquiring more Seeds of Possibility. Was the easiest route to shoot for the Susano Martial Arts Academy event dungeon? I could probably get them from the Amaterasu Academy event, too, but that was still a long way down the line, and I'd rather steer clear of it if possible. Maybe Iori could deal with it for me somehow.

I also knew of another place I could head to immediately. The only issue was that it was almost guaranteed to be more difficult than my solo forty-layer challenge in the Academy Dungeon, even with Yukine and company tagging along to help. There was one other place I could get ahold of them beyond that, too.

Marino closed her eyes and pinched the bridge of her nose before letting out a long sigh. After a short moment, she lifted her face up and grinned.

"Thanks a bunch, Kou! ♪ But I actually don't need one. The thing is, using one of those wouldn't do anything for me."

I pondered her words. It wouldn't "do anything for her"? Did that mean……?

My attempts to think about the deeper implications of her statement were immediately dashed when Marino closed in and gave me a hug.

She quickly separated herself from me and flashed a gentle smile. How pillowy soft they were.

"I'm very happy to hear you were planning on giving one to me, you know. Those seeds are an expensive commodity. They're worth more than you could possibly imagine."

"...They are?"

"Absolutely, which is all the more reason why I think you'll have a hard time getting people to accept them from you. It might be best to avoid saying anything and trick them into eating them instead."

"Force them to take the seeds without telling them first? I don't know, that's going to be tough."

"They aren't that big, right? Couldn't you mix them in with something?"

That did seem like it could work, but...

"You can always come to me if you need some camouflage, okay?"

"Putting that on hold for now... I still want to give one to either Sis or Claris..."

"Oh, right, you mentioned that. Go ahead and give it to Claris. Hatsumi…would probably say she doesn't need it, or that she'd be fine waiting until later."

"...You think so?"

"Personally, I think you'd be fine making her wait, too."

"Why?"

"Because Hatsumi honestly doesn't seem to want to get stronger. Though it seems like she's reconsidering lately."

When Marino put it like that, I agreed that Sis wasn't inclined to get more power of her own.

"You might not know this yet Kousuke, but Hatsumi's very, very powerful. Even if you teamed up with Claris, Yukine, and Ludie against her, it would be a while before you would all be able to take her down, I think."

I thought I had misheard her at first.

We couldn't beat Sis? I admit that Yukine hadn't gotten strong enough yet to live up to her status as one of *Magical★Explorer's* Big Three. Unlike President Monica, who is stupidly strong from the moment she joins your party, or the Founding Saint, who has all sorts of bizarre things going on from the start, her strength starts out middling.

Still, I felt like Yukine should at least be relatively powerful by this point. She could even use Nine-Headed Dragon. Would teaming up with Claris really not be enough to bring Sis down?

I had sparred with Sis on numerous occasions by now, and she'd defeated me with a barrage of magic each time. Was that move alone enough to send not just me, but Claris, Ludie, and Yukine out of commission, too?

"Hatsumi's *strong*. I'm not joking. She's still got a long way to go compared to me, though."

Sis wasn't one of the heroines, so I had no idea what her in-game stats were like.

But wait a minute. In-game, Sis is tasked with the important job of teaching powerful spells to Iori. Super overpowered magic that felt like cheating. It wouldn't make sense if she couldn't use the magic she taught to Iori herself, right? No, that couldn't possibly be the case.

I mean, for starters, Sis...

"So if you're handing out that last seed, I think Claris would be the better choice. I don't know if she'd accept it or not, mind you. Go ahead and ask Hatsumi first if you're really worried about her."

"Okay......"

There were too many things to think about: Marino, Sis, the larger Hanamura family, and the possibility that they were all somehow connected to me, too.

"Oh, right, I almost forgot. Can we go back to your nighttime rendezvous plans for tonight?"

"Sure.........Wait, what?"

"I'd be careful about going to visit people willy-nilly; it seems like Hatsumi's been sleeping in a different room lately."

I couldn't hold back a sigh.

Marino grinned. "It seems like she's never in her room when I drop by." But she clearly knew what was really going on. I couldn't take her comment any other way.

Sis was usually in my room, after all...

After chatting with Marino for a short while longer, I left. To get my jumbled thoughts in order, I decided to go up the stairs and head for my room for the time being. Along the way, however, the door to Nanami's quarters clicked open, out of which emerged Sis.

............From Nanami's room?

"Oh, Sis."

"Mm."

Sis was expressionless as ever, but she somehow looked sleepier than usual, like she was going to flop into bed the moment she got back to her room. I took that as a signal to talk things through with her first.

"Can I speak with you for a bit before bed, Sis?"

"Okay."

"Great... Let's go somewhere we can chat instead of standing here."

Nodding, Sis briskly walked to my room and opened the door without a second thought. She then moved Marianne, the stuffed orca that was currently occupying my desk chair, to my bed, and reached for my electric kettle to make us some tea.

Just as I went to stop Sis and insist on brewing it myself, a thought crossed my mind.

Hang on, this is *my room, right?*

Ludie and Nanami would also do this sort of thing. With all these girls making themselves at home in here, it felt like my room was basically their room. Not that I had any issue with it...

"What did you want to talk about?"

Sis's question brought me back to reality.

"Right, right."

Pouring a cup of chamomile tea and passing it to Sis, I took out the Seed of Possibility.

"I've never seen one of these before. How pretty."

"Yeah...... It's called a Seed of Possibility."

Her face fell for just a second.

"Amazing, good job finding it. Where was it?"

"Thanks. I got it in the Academy Dungeon...and there's something I need to apologize to you about, Sis."

▶ Chapter 2: Seeds of Possibility

"Apologize? Why?"

What I wanted to get across was that I was going to give her one of the seeds later, and that I wanted her to wait for the time being. That was all. Yet our conversation ended up covering a lot more ground than I expected.

I was attempting to express my gratitude to her.

Sis was always indirectly helping me and looking out for me however she could.

While we were talking, it surprised me how involved the conversation got. We discussed all sorts of things. Sis's favorite movies, her favorite books. Even my favorite things to watch and read, too.

After taking that long detour, I finally told her, "I want to give a seed to you, too, Sis. The next time I find one, I promise I'll give it to you no matter what, so just wait it out for me."

She smiled, squinting.

Sis finished off the rest of her chamomile tea before slowly coming over to sit beside me.

Then she pulled my neck and head toward her.

"Thank you, but I can wait until later. I don't want it that much, so I can go without it."

"Huh, but—"

"I have you here, Kousuke, so I don't need it."

Still hugging me close, she stroked my head before eventually announcing it was time for bed. She undressed down to her underwear, then finally got into bed and cuddled Marianne.

I watched this play out in bewilderment, my shock as big as her chest, but I couldn't resist getting one last mental quip in.

Sis? The bed and Marianne are both *mine*, you know.

I left my room and made my way to Ludie's. She greeted me in her pajamas, though it appeared she hadn't gone to sleep yet.

"What are you doing here so late?"

"Um, well, it's no big deal…"

She encouraged me to sit, and I plopped down on her green sofa.

Almost everything in Ludie's room was the same shade of green she liked. From the curtains to her bedding to the sofa.

Ludie must have been relaxing before bed, because she placed a bookmark in a novel and set it aside after she beckoned me in. Dressed in a simple white negligee featuring adorable frills, she emanated a bizarre combination of eroticism and elegant beauty.

"I just had something to give you."

"Give me?"

"Yup, right here."

I took out three small shining golden seeds from the pouch I'd brought with me.

"What are these?"

"They're, uhhh, tasty treats! Just pop them into your...... Sorry."

My excuse sounded ridiculous even as it left my lips. Ludie must've felt the same, because her gaze sharpened into a glare as I spoke.

"...That's obviously not true, right?"

"Yeaaah, you got me."

"So spill it. What are these?"

Ludie gently picked up one of the seeds and sighed slightly.

"They're called Seeds of Possibility..."

She was examining the seeds reflecting in the light when she jumped in surprise, which caught me off guard. Her eyes turning into saucers, she gently placed the seed back on the table, as if she was handling an antique tea bowl worth hundreds of thousands of dollars.

"What're you making me hold here?!"

"I mean, I didn't *make* you do it..."

She was the one who'd picked them up herself.

"Are these the real thing? You weren't taken in by a fake, were you?"

"They're authentic enough to make Marino and Nanami quit their silly jokes and talk seriously for a moment."

Ludie's look grew even sterner.

When I went to continue speaking, she put her hand up to stop me.

"...Wait. Let me calm down a moment."

She closed her eyes and took a deep breath. Then, with her eyes still shut, she put away the book she'd placed beside the chair and sat up straight. The refinement of each movement reminded me that she really was a member of the nobility.

Ludie slowly opened her eyes.

"Better. Go ahead."

"I want to give this to you."

"What?!"

She widened her eyes in shock.

"Wait a minute! You're giving it to me instead of using it on yourself or selling it?!"

She shot me a look that made the words, *What's wrong with you, stupid!* echo in my head.

"I already took one. I actually got five of them, see. I figured I'd give one to everyone who's helped me out."

"Wait, I'm not following any of this."

"I want to give this to you, Ludie."

I repeated this to her one more time.

"Please, just hold on. I couldn't possibly accept something like this!! Do you know just how much one of these things is worth?! Besides, you're the one always doing things for me, so how could I possible accept something as priceless as this?!"

"But you've given me so many things I can't put a price on, either, Ludie. I mean, this doesn't even begin to pay you back…"

"………Have I really given you anything like that?"

"Sure have. Not only that, but it helped me out so much I……well, it's pretty embarrassing to say this face-to-face, but, um, those forty layers ended up being pretty tough after all…"

"Of course they were, stupid! Yukine and the others even told you that it would normally be impossible."

The way she phrased it made me sound abnormal, but I guess she was right.

"Well…the thing is, when I was thinking to myself, 'Whew, I don't know if I'm gonna make it,' I looked at the charm you gave me and felt this strange power kinda surge up inside me. Without it, I probably would've given up in the latter half of the thirtieth layer, I think. Your gift supported me when I needed it the most."

At this, I took out the slightly misshapen protective charm Ludie had given me.

Then I dangled it gently in front of her to show it off.

"H-hold on now… Wait. Wait, wait, wait. Wh-what are you talking about?! And put that thing away. It's super embarrassing!"

Flustered, Ludie leaned forward to try and grab the charm. However, I had no intention of handing over my treasure. I immediately moved it out of Ludie's reach but kept it in view.

"I'm pretty embarrassed, too, actually."

"Then put it away, dummy! First of all, that thing isn't worth nearly as much as a Seed of Protection! Yukine gave me the fabric for it, so the amount of money it took for me to make it wouldn't even cover a cup of instant ramen!"

"Sure, I get that it might've been cheap to create, but... That's not what makes something valuable, right? That's why your charm is much more precious to me than those seeds."

Her face went beet red. I figured my face was probably just as flushed by that point.

"I feel bad that these seeds are all I have to repay you with, but will you take one for me?"

"'These seeds'? You've got some nerve... I haven't even paid you back for the ring you gave me."

Her face still crimson, Ludie remained hesitant to accept the seed I'd offered her.

"Hey, Ludie?"

"What?"

"I told you something before I went into the Academy Dungeon, right?"

"Told me what?"

"That I wanted you to explore with me from here on out. And, well... I'd like you to put aside your objections for a moment and just listen to everything I want to say. That all right?"

"When you put it like that, it only makes me more worried. Fine."

"The thing is, one of my goals is clearing the entirety of the Academy Dungeon."

Ludie nodded without saying a word.

"And I'm absolutely gonna need everyone's strength to make that happen."

I was obviously going to need Detect Traps while charting the labyrinth, and I couldn't go without long-range magic, support magic, and healing magic in combat. But that wasn't the whole story. There was the mental aspect of having people help you out, too.

"So I feel a bit guilty, but I'd really like it if, um, you know, you could always come along with me."

"Don't be—don't feel guilty. I'll...I'll go with you."

"Thanks. But hold on, just listen a bit longer. The thing is, I'll admit that you're already strong, seed or no seed, and I think you're only gonna get even more powerful."

▶ Chapter 2: Seeds of Possibility 25

 Watching Ludie rapidly improve and hone her abilities had assured me of this. That said, if we wound up fighting against each other in a mock battle or something, I wasn't planning on losing to her, either.
 "But since I'm going to be clearing dungeons with everyone? I figured everyone should get as strong as they possibly can. That goes for Nanami and Yukine, too."
 Ludie wouldn't just remove the limits on her stat growth by ingesting a Seed of Possibility. She'd also gain an aptitude for healing and support magic, and beyond that, she would be able to learn even more spells.
 Ludie's power would skyrocket. No doubt about it.
 "A mutually advantageous arrangement, right? But above all else…"
 "Yes?"
 "…………I think it would be really nice for us both to gain this potential and grow stronger together. How great it'd be to reach the deepest floor of the dungeon together, you know?"
 "……You idiot. Fine, fine, I get it, okay?" Ludie replied, taking one of the seeds and staring at me.
 "I also want to get more powerful, though probably not as much as you do. But more than that…"
 At first, I thought she had cast a spell on me.
 Ludie squinted slightly and smiled warmly. Simple as that.
 But her expression was brimming with a mystical charm that seemed capable of making even Narcissus, cursed to love only himself, fall for her.
 "I want to see it all together."
 Ludie gulped down the seed.
 My heart was pounding in my chest. But since I was feeling a bit bashful, I tried to pretend as if it was no big deal, just barely getting out a "Yeah, let's work hard together."
 Ludie also seemed embarrassed; she broke eye contact and turned her still-flushed cheeks away from me.
 Feigning composure to mask my thundering heartbeat, I looked at Ludie, her head slightly tilted down to the floor, and changed the subject.
 "Oh right, I almost forgot."
 "……What now?"
 "Ramen trip this weekend? That place by the station?"

"……Sure, but you're paying."

"Oh, and once I'm done with my training tomorrow? I'd love a massage. For free of course. I mean, since I'm treating you to ramen, right?"

"*Hee-hee*, hmm, a massage, you say."

Looking a bit proud as she spoke, Ludie turned to me with a full-faced grin.

"I don't mind giving you one, but… The ramen this weekend's a different matter entirely. You better bring me a cup of instant noodles if you want a massage."

I couldn't help but chuckle and remark about how much of a ramen maniac this girl was. Ludie incredulously asked what was wrong with liking ramen, and the two of us shared in a few moments of laughter.

My last destination was Yukine's room. She had started occupying it at one point or another and had since claimed it for herself.

"Sorry, this is the only one I have," Yukine said, bringing me a cup of tea. On top of the lacquered saucer was an awkwardly misshapen teacup.

I took a sip and let out a sigh after savoring the gentle bitterness.

Yukine had readily showed me into her room when I'd showed up at her door asking to talk.

It was very much like her that, despite my sudden visit, she prepared a cup of tea for me without being asked.

"*Heh-heh*, make yourself at home."

"Thank you," I replied before adjusting my position on the floor cushion.

Yukine's room had been pretty drab before I'd delved into the Academy Dungeon. She seemed to be accumulating more and more belongings by the day, though, so the space was rapidly acquiring a lived-in feel.

I didn't recall the tatami mat or floor cushions being here the last time I visited.

"Oh, this…… Nanami actually set it up for me. I mean, I wanted one, and before I knew it, she had laid it out… Though I don't remember ever telling her I was interested in it," Yukine said, stroking the tatami mat. She must have picked up on my eyes wandering from the cushions to the floor.

Though she was the type to come up to you with a goofy pose and a straight face, Nanami was a capable servant, both inside the dungeon and out.

"You said you had something to discuss, right, Takioto? Actually, I went to your room just a moment ago because I had something to speak with you about, but…"

I nodded knowingly.

"Ah, sorry. No one came to the door, right? I was out visiting Ludie and Marino's rooms."

"No, uh…about that… Ms. Hatsumi came to the door instead. She looked like she'd just woken up."

…………

Words escaped me. I unconsciously heaved a sigh and put my face in my hands.

"So, erm… Just what sort of relationship do you have with her…? I don't know if it's actually okay to ask you that, but I just couldn't help but wonder, is the thing…"

"You've seen me sleeping on the sofa before, though, right?"

Yukine panicked and froze for a moment. Then she gave an audible "Oooh."

"R-right. I think I can guess the rest. You have it rough."

"I've gotten used to it."

I figured it was best to avoid mentioning that we did share the same bed on occasion.

"W-well in that case, you can use my room if you want, too. I-I'm used to sleeping on a futon mattress on the floor anyway, so I can just lay it out here."

"Ah, sorry for making you worry. I'll be…"

"Hm? So I could use her bed?"

"Wha?"

"Yeah, I don't mind."

O-okay, now hold on a minute. Was that really going to be okay?

The sheets that wrapped around those empyreal peaks—full of charm, voluptuous, sexy, erotic, arousing; around the beautiful porcelain nape of her neck, which always drew my eyes during our runs; around her supple, perfectly sculpted butt that was just the right size. Sheets filled with Yukine's scent. And by inviting a gentleman like me inside, her sublime—

"Takioto! Takioto!"

"Yes, I'm here!"

"Wh-what happened? You looked like you were staring off into another dimension!"

"Oh, uh. I-it's nothing."

I needed to calm down.

Yukine was simply looking out for me and trying to help.

That said, there was a laundry list of reasons why I wouldn't be able to fall asleep in her bed. Heck, I'd probably count over a million sheep before I could get myself to nod off if she was snoozing on the floor right next to me.

I was certain the night hours would feel like an eternity, leaving me in agony until the morning sun washed over, ensuring I'd be facing my dungeon runs with bloodshot eyes.

Definitely not ideal.

"Thanks but no thanks. I'll be okay. Part of me would give up an arm just to get a shot at sleeping in your bed, but…I can't let myself put you out like that."

"Just how backed against the wall are you, here?"

"I'm okay. I promise."

Borrowing her bed would be the *not* okay option in many ways, despite the fact that I wanted it more than anything. On the other hand, maybe that wouldn't be a good solution after all… Yup, I didn't really understand the point I was getting at.

"Well, you can come to me anytime, okay? Now then. Let's start with you, Takioto."

"Ah, right. There's something I'd like to give you."

I had Yukine hold out her hand, and I placed one of the golden seeds into her palm.

"………What is this?"

"I figure that you've probably heard about these before. It's called a Seed of Possibility, and—"

"Hold on a minute!"

Yukine frantically tried to return the seed to my hands, but I hid them behind my back.

"What in the world are you thinking, giving me something like this?"

"Yukine, these seeds are why I made that solo trip into the Academy Dungeon."

Like someone scoping out a burglary, she shifted her eyes from the seed to me then back at the seed, placing her head in her hands and glancing every which way. Ludie had acted similarly, so I got the feeling this must have been the average reaction to seeing a Seed of Possibility.

"Hold up, you worked hard to get these, right? You should use it on yourself."

"Already did. I came by several of them at once. That's why I want to make sure the people who helped me get this far, like you and Ludie, also get one."

"...You could build a castle anywhere you wanted with this."

Was this thing really worth that much?

"Then I guess *this* easily eclipses a palace in value. I couldn't begin to put a price on it," I said, producing the charm that Yukine had made for me.

"D-don't be stupid... That thing isn't worth anything."

Did it really seem that way? It definitely didn't to me.

"No, it's worth something to me. Compared to this charm, that seed is worth about as much as a gum wrapper."

Out of either embarrassment or joy—or both—Yukine blushed slightly when I said this, then hid her mouth with the back of her hand and turned away.

"You can't put a price on that charm, and it isn't the only invaluable thing you've given me. The same goes for the moves I make in battle—the teachings and training that I've gotten from you and Claris dwell in each and every one. If you two hadn't been there to spar with me, I doubt I would have been able to clear those forty floors."

In the worst-case scenario, I might not have been able to make it back home at all.

"I've already given one to Nanami and Ludie, too, given how much they've worked with me. I'd like to do the same for you, Yukine."

"But..."

"What you've done for me is worth so much more than what it'd cost to build some castle on primo real estate—that's how much strength you've given me, Yukine. That's why I want to thank you. If anything, it feels like this might still be lacking. Please, take it."

She looked down at the seed in her hands, her expression still solemn.

"You're really not going to regret giving this to me?"

"No. I truly would like you to have it."

Yukine sighed slightly and glanced at the ceiling. Then she looked back at me, her expression serious, but her face pink.

"You said you wanted to become the strongest out there, right, Takioto?"

"I sure did."

"Are you certain about this? Giving me one of these?"

"Of course. I want you to get stronger, too."

Her reservation made sense in that I might indeed lose to her eventually. But that wasn't what I was after.

My real goal was a storybook ending. I wanted it so badly that I'd give one to Iori, Katorina, and all my classmates, along with all the members of the Three Committees, too.

But above all else.

I believed that the Yukine Mizumori who became one of the Big Three, a cut above the rest, was the best Yukine Mizumori of all. I wanted the upperclassman I loved so much to…

"Surpass me and become the strongest."

Looking at Yukine, who seemed to be seriously thinking something over, I spoke up, spurred by a need to break the silence somehow.

"Besides… Th-this serves my own self-interests, too… If I give you this, I figure you'll go dungeon diving with me…and help me out with my training and stuff as well…"

"I was planning on partying up with you regardless of whether you gave me something like this, you know. The same for helping you train, too. As long as you want it."

Yukine stared hard at the seed in her hand.

"It feels like I'm very—deeply, even—indebted to you now…"

"Then this'll cancel everything out. 'Cause I felt deeply indebted to you already," I replied before taking out my charm.

"Dummy. That doesn't compare to this at all."

"You're right about that. Your charm is far more precious to me, after all. A priceless treasure."

"…You really are something, I swear," Yukine replied, as if squeezing the words out of her throat. Then her cheeks reddened, and she averted her gaze, hiding her smile with the back of her hand.

A few moments later, she swallowed the Seed of Possibility.

Then she directed a happy grin my way. A smile that made my whole body feel full just looking at it, like my feelings were going to come bursting out of me.

Seeing Yukine look so pleased made me happy in turn.

"I hope you'll keep helping me from here on out, Yukine."

"You bet. I'm going into dungeons with you even if you say you don't need me, got it? And I'll work you to the bone in training from here on out, too. Not only that..."

"There's more?"

"You might eclipse me and become the strongest yourself. But I'm not going to give you an easy run at it, you hear me?"

This must have been her declaration of war. I only had one answer.

"I wouldn't have it any other way."

Yukine and I smiled as we looked each other in the eye. It was a very cozy moment.

As I stared at Yukine, her expression changed abruptly.

"Right. I...I have something to talk to you about, too, Takioto."

"Oh yeah, you mentioned that."

She'd tried to bring it up before her unfortunate run-in with Sis.

"I have something to give you as well, but that's about where the similarities end."

"Something to give me? What is it?"

"Yes. Though it's absolutely worthless compared to what you gave me..."

"Um, Yukine?" I replied, taking out the charm again.

"I-I get it, I get it. Th-that's, um—it's embarrassing, so put it away. Wh-why're you keeping it so carefully tucked away in your chest pocket, anyway?!"

"Because it's very important to me, of course."

Yukine cleared her throat after a few moments, but her face was still tinged pink.

She reached inside her pocket and took out an elegant purple cloth. She unfolded it and produced a single letter from inside.

"What's this?"

Taking the letter in my hands, I flipped it over.

I saw the magical circle and the seal of the Academy written on it and felt my hands shake slightly.

In an extremely unfortunate turn of events, it was not, in fact, a love letter from Yukine. Compared to that, it was something almost laughably trivial.

But it was still something I had wanted.

I touched the magic circle on the back of the letter and sent mana into it.

When I did, the insignias of the Student Council, the Morals Committee, and the Ceremonial Committee floated into the air, and the letter opened on its own.

Just as a single card flew out of it, Yukine began to speak.

"Congratulations, Kousuke Takioto. You've been chosen."

I couldn't believe that I was actually hearing this line spoken in real life. In the game, one of the Three Committee vice presidents does this, but they must have entrusted it to Yukine Mizumori this time, given that she'd been in contact with me the most out of the other committee members. It was a completely insignificant line, one I'd heard so many times across my playthroughs of the game that I felt like skipping it.

I never would have thought that this line and letter would bring me so much joy.

"So the time's finally come, huh…"

There appeared to be something written on the card, but I didn't need to read it to know what it said.

It was a fervent request from the Three Committees.

Chapter 3: The Three Committees

"Why, that went far better than I could've expected..."

"You're the one who proposed the idea, so why're you the most surprised here?"

Ludie, who'd been speaking like a prim and proper young noblewoman, smiled dryly at my reply.

Her aristocratic facade was unavoidable at the moment. It was school commuting hours, and there were students in the area. For the past few minutes, I'd noticed people occasionally sneaking peeks at us. This time around, however, they might have been paying more attention to me than her.

"But she would've definitely shot me down if I tried to give it to her like usual."

"I don't think even a direct order from myself would've done the trick."

This opinion wasn't only shared by Ludie and me. The funny thing was that Sis, Marino, Nanami, and Yukine had all felt the same way, too. That being said, Yukine had hesitated a little when it came time to put words into action—until we finally convinced her that there wasn't really any other option.

Everyone had been very on board while getting everything ready, especially Marino, who'd clearly enjoyed it as a fun activity. Though I had to hand it to her—the whole thing had gone off without a hitch thanks to how perfectly she'd played her role, which was central to the operation's success.

"Well, I figured it would be tough going, but...ultimately, I thought things would end up like this......... Is something the matter?"

"Oh no. I suppose not."

Ludie's mannerisms and way of speaking felt wholly incongruous. She must have picked up on my discomfort from my reaction.

Since I hadn't been in the Academy lately, it was my first time seeing Ludie in princess mode in quite a while. Plus, I had been in the dungeon the past four days, so I hadn't really interacted with anyone.

"But how does she feel now that it's actually happened? Is she upset?"

"I believe it would depend on the time and place. This time, I imagine she'll be grateful in the end."

"I agree with Miss Ludie," Nanami said, following behind us at an angle.

"According to the information I've acquired, she seemed to be panicked about seeing both Master and Miss Ludie's exponential growth."

"She never once told me as much, though...," Ludie said, knitting her brows slightly in displeasure.

But if she really had been worried about it, she wouldn't have said anything about it to Ludie. She would've kept it locked inside. And how exactly did Nanami know that, anyway? I'd had the same thought back when I helped out Yukine. It was a total mystery where that maid got her information.

"How the heck did you figure that out...?"

"Well, I tempted the person in question with fruit wine, and once I drank her under the table, I learned everything I wanted to know in one stroke."

Now I got it. So she had a weakness for fruit wine. The "everything" and "one stroke" turns of phrase raised alarm bells in my head, but I tried my best to flush it from my consciousness and forget about it.

"If you're just listening to her whine and complain, that's fine, but try not to go overboard."

Nanami had been proving almost frighteningly capable and competent lately, but she'd still get up to something weird every now and then. At times like these, I needed to be firm and—

"Worry not, Master. I made sure to ask about her taste in men and what her body measurements are."

—reward her for a job well down. What a truly exceptional maid. I could search to the edge of the world and back without finding a maid more wonderful, more fantastic than—

"*Hrk...!*"

"Takioto, we're almost at school."

"Got it..."

Um, Ludie? Nanami was clearly joking, okay? So, uh, I don't think it was necessary to elbow me in the stomach like that.

We continued onto the campus grounds, turning heads as we made our way to our classroom. When I opened the door and stepped inside, I found all my classmates dumbstruck. Some even did a double take when they saw me.

"Jeez, if you're here, Takioto, then I bet the sky'll be full of pigs tomorrow."

That was the first thing he had to say to me? Orange stared at me hard in the face as he made his remark.

"Hey, the hell's that supposed to mean?"

"C'mon, man. I haven't seen you in class *at all* lately."

"Sure, you might not see me in the classroom... But we still have lunch together every once in a while, so you've seen me more than everyone else here..."

Though he wasn't exactly wrong. Since the start of midterms, heck, even before then, I'd been skipping most of my real classes. If I did come to school, it was either for lunch or to head into one of the dungeons.

Today was no exception, and if I didn't have something planned in the afternoon, I probably would have made straight for the dungeon instead of coming to campus.

"And I still don't think that warrants looking at me like you've seen a ghost or something," I replied, purposefully raising my voice and tilting my head. The girl with a bob-cut turned around and casually apologized, bringing her hands together with a smile.

Truth was, I couldn't have been any more grateful. It was thanks to Ludie and Iori's efforts that I could relish this silly everyday banter. Outside this room, I was the center of attention.

When I walked through the campus, a path would part before me. The first-years would avoid me, the second- and third-years would whisper, "That must be him, right?" to each other, and the members of LLL would look at me with a mixture of dread and envy.

And on top of all that...... I glanced over at Nanami.

She was standing expressionlessly next to Ludie but winked when she noticed my stare. Tactful. While I was in the middle of talking with the other guys, she'd distanced herself from the conversation. She'd made friends with the other *Magical★Explorer* heroines—not just Ludie, but Katorina and Class Rep, too—somewhere down the line and was having a normal conversation with them.

I felt like she'd finally started getting fans of her own recently.

Whenever we walked somewhere, I'd spy male students looking her way and letting out a sigh.

Nanami was indeed beautiful. Her silky-smooth silver hair might have put her stunning features ahead of Ludie's, depending on who was looking. Her body was well-toned, despite the fact that she had such huge breasts—though not as big as Sis's. Coupled with her plump, shapely butt, she struck quite the dynamic figure.

But her maid uniform was what really sealed the deal. It brought the appeal of her other features to a whole different level.

I didn't blame anyone for being unable to take their eyes off her. Nor did I blame anyone for lobbing looks of jealousy my way for savoring her service.

But I knew for certain those annoying stares would become unbearable if they continued in the classroom. Although I could ignore it all to some extent, just the thought of getting scrutinized in this small, enclosed space was enough to get me down. Ludie insisted that I'd get used it, but I wondered when that state of peaceful enlightenment was supposed to come my way.

"By the way, Takioto, there's something that's been bothering me…," the bob-haired girl began tentatively.

"What's up?"

"So, um, that stuff about being the relative of Principal Hanamura… is that true?"

"Oh, I was also wondering about that!"

A bit taken aback by the question, I eyed the girl who had jumped into the conversation.

Iori's younger stepsister, Yuika Hijiri. She had bright, twinkling eyes, and she'd gathered her hair into a side ponytail. Her chest was reasonably large, and her mannerisms were as adorable as a puppy dog's.

"Wait, Yuika?"

Iori asked where she'd popped up from, but Yuika sidestepped the question.

"You want to know too, right?"

▶ Chapter 3: The Three Committees

"I mean, I guess," Iori said with a strained smile.

"Oh, so the Hanamura family stuff. I wasn't really hiding it or anything, but my mom's actually Marino's cousin. Her maiden name was Hanamura. Sis—er, I mean, Ms. Hatsumi would be my second cousin."

Both of Yuika's eyes bulged, and she practically shouted with surprise, while my classmate seemed put off somehow by my reply.

"Wait, 'Sis'? Really.........? So you were born with a silver spoon after all."

Orange looked at me enviously.

Yuika, her eyes sparkling, repeated over and over again how amazing the revelation was.

Judging by how they spoke to me, it seemed that everyone imagined I had the upbringing of a spoiled royal brat. But if that applied to anyone here, it was Ludie. Meanwhile, Takioto had traversed a life of turmoil. Not that anyone could tell.

But I didn't need to go to the effort of explaining that. Then I'd have to talk about how my parents were both dead, and then I'd need to mention that I was now living at Marino's house. Depending on how the conversation played out, there was a chance they'd find out Ludie was also living there, too.

"C'mon then, Takioto. Treat us to something."

I didn't hesitate to shake my head at the bob-haired girl's comment.

"Whoa, there. If that's gonna be how it is, then go earn that money in a dungeon instead... I can give you some recs."

"For real? That's totally good enough. I'd be psyched to hear them!" she replied, surprised.

She must not have actually expected to get anything.

"Ooh, I want those, too!" Yuika said right after the other girl.

She pulled at my arm, a big, adorable grin on her face. I could feel them so clearly, rubbing right up against me, and I definitely didn't mind one bit.

"That's okay, right?"

"Yeah, sure."

Of course it was okay.

At that same moment, a question came to mind.

Why was Yuika being so aggressive and intense in her approach? It's true that Yuika treats Takioto a lot better than the other heroines do in *MX*. But does anyone ever hit on him?

What was making her act like this, then? I thought about the differences between who I was now and the Takioto of the game......and didn't even know where to start.

The most significant differences were likely the Hanamura family stuff and the fact that I'd gotten first in my grade. But that alone was more than enough to explain her treatment of me.

"You've already taught us a whole bunch, anyway...... Right, Orange?"

"For sure. Like that dungeon we went to the other day. Kousuke told you about that place, right?"

"Oh, how'd it go? I figured it'd be easy to farm there."

"It was fantastic!" Iori cheerfully replied, eyes sparkling.

"G-great."

All I had done was introduce him to a random dungeon, so I felt a bit embarrassed to see him overjoyed by it. But if that was how he was going to be, then I just needed to tell him about an even better dungeon next time, didn't I?

"By the way, what are you up to this afternoon? There's something I wanted to go over with ya."

It was Orange who asked for my help. Maybe he had hit a bit of a plateau? I didn't mind listening to what he had to say, but...

"Ah, sorry, but I got somewhere to be today."

"Seriously? Where?"

"The Moon Court."

Even Orange was familiar with that location by the looks of it.

Almost everyone seemed astonished, so they must have surmised the implications.

Seeing the current situation in front of me made me realize... it was probably better if I got everyone on the same page while I could.

"Huh, what's the Moon Court?" Yuika asked, cocking her head. She was the only person there who didn't understand the significance of the name.

"Here at this Academy, we actually have these three organizations that hold a loooot of power on campus. They're the Student Council, the Morals Committee, and the Ceremonial Committee."

Iori was the one to reply.

"And these three committees? They're special groups that only students with exceptional abilities are allowed to join."

"Huh, I didn't know about that."

"Right, and the thing is…"

Iori's eyes, and the eyes of all my classmates nearby, settled on me.

"The Moon Court is the Three Committee's base of operations. The average student wouldn't be allowed inside at all."

Tsukuyomi Academy's Moon Court was a unique area that only members of the Three Committees could enter, for the most part. Regular students could get into some floors if they were given permission. However, the only people who could advance farther into the inner areas of the Moon Court were the members of the Three Committees and a certain subset of the instructors.

Naturally, I'd never seen it or been inside before. I had visited it a number of times in-game, but it would've raised suspicion if I was suddenly summoned there and knew the way around perfectly. That was all the more reason why Yukine had proposed to guide me.

"Sorry for keeping you, Yukine."

"What do you mean? You're five minutes early, aren't you? I only just got here a few minutes ago. That said…"

Yukine's gaze drifted to Nanami. It was natural to wonder why she was here. Heck, even I was surprised by it.

"I will absolutely be accompanying him."

"So she says. She's even gotten permission from Marino…"

At this, Nanami reached inside her cleavage and pulled out a card with the academy crest on it. I had never seen it in the game before, nor had I seen it since coming to this world, either.

…But the question was, why did she put it in there? She definitely made sure I got a good view of her cleavage when she took it out, too. Hey, Nanami, listen, you don't need to act like one of those overly sultry anime characters, okay?

Though it was super sexy.

"*Ha-ha-ha*… All right, it shouldn't be a problem. I'll be with you anyway, so I'm sure it's fine. Let's get moving, then."

Yukine smiled awkwardly, and Nanami and I followed behind her into the teleportation circle.

On the other side was what could be described as a sort of tiny palace.

Before us was a garden with a beautiful array of flowers in full bloom, a fountain at its center, and white chairs and tables laid out nearby.

While the scene didn't throw me off too much since I'd already experienced the Hanamura house, I was sure a regular student would find it overwhelming.

Yukine urged us forward, and Nanami and I took a step inside the palace walls. As we walked down a hall adorned with dazzling and gorgeous decorations, I quietly took a deep breath. Then, repeatedly opening and closing both my fists, I started relaxing the excess tension in my body as best I could.

After a short while, Yukine stopped in front of a big door with the school crest engraved on it.

I started doing deep breathing again when I noticed a tap on my back. Then I reflexively turned around and felt a tiny prick on my face.

Nanami was digging her finger into my cheek.

I couldn't suppress a dry smile as I looked at her smug grin.

"Takioto."

Before I could say anything to Nanami, Yukine drew my attention, so I turned back toward her.

When I did, I found another small prick on the face waiting for me. Yukine was digging her finger into my cheek.

"Not you too…"

All I could do was laugh.

To be honest, I was a little nervous. Both because of the atmosphere of this place and from imagining what awaited me on the other side of this door. That was why I was seriously grateful for their little prank, as it helped ease some of the tension.

"Sorry, I couldn't help myself."

"Fine then, I suppose I can allow it, just this once."

What a way to phrase things after she did such a great job easing my nerves.

"*Ha-ha-ha*," Yukine laughed. Nanami didn't actually say anything, but she wore a triumphant smile on her face.

After a brief pause, Yukine asked me, "Ready?"

I nodded, and she opened the door.

Inside the room, the most important people of the afternoon were already seated.

On the right side was the Ceremonial Minister of the Ceremonial

Committee, Benito Evangelista, along with the disarmingly smiling Vice Minister, Shion Himemiya. Behind them was a wall displaying the insignias for the Student Council, Morals Committee, and Ceremonial Committee.

On the left side was the Morals Committee Captain, Saint Stefania Scaglione. Yukine walked over to her side.

In front of me, staring at me with her arms crossed, was the Student Council President, Monica Mercedes von Mobius, as well as the Vice President, Franziska Edda von Gneisenau, who adjusted her glasses when our eyes met.

President Monica stood up from her seat when Yukine called out to her.

"Good day to you, Takioto. And you as well, Nanami."

"It appears you are familiar with me, but allow me to introduce myself. I am the supremely and stunningly beautiful maid, Nanami."

She curtsied. Well, seeing that she stuck out like a sore thumb, it was probably a given that they'd know who she was. That, and she had already encountered Vice President Fran before.

I felt like Nanami had given a pretty wild self-introduction, but the committee members' reactions were decidedly unperturbed.

Vice President Fran prefaced her comment with, "I do apologize, but..." and looked at Nanami. "As a rule, only a select few people are allowed to listen to what's talked about here. We cannot let someone who is neither an instructor nor a member of the Three Committees be privy to our conversation."

However, Nanami shook her head at Fran's instructions.

"That won't be a problem," she said before taking a card out of her pocket. Seeing this, Minister Benito whistled.

"Wow, isn't that something."

"Why, this is my first time seeing one for myself. Though I do suppose she is a Hanamura maid, yes?"

"Please pardon me for interjecting. I would like to make one thing clear: I serve Master Kousuke Takioto, not the Hanamura family. I have nothing to do with that old hag Marino, and I ask for your understanding on this point."

"'Old hag'...?"

Vice President Fran was at a loss for words. Meanwhile, Yukine wore a strained smile. The Ceremonial Committee members looked to be enjoying themselves. President Monica's expression remained unchanged, along with Saint Stef's.

"Oh yes, I thoroughly understand now. So it's Takioto you work for, not the Hanamuras, hmm?" Shion said, smirking.

"Time to get down to business, Shion," Yukine said, prompting the other woman to open her fan and place it up to her mouth. However, it was clear from the look in her eyes that she was still grinning.

"A bit surprised, are you? Seeing the Ceremonial Committee and the Student Council chatting so congenially like this, I mean. Or maybe you knew about that?"

Naturally I knew all about it. When I smiled, President Monica nodded.

"Well, how about the Ceremonial Committee, then?" Minister Benito chimed in. "My, Takioto. You've climbed up the ranks several times faster than I could've imagined."

"It's good to see you again, Minister Benito Evangelista. I'm aware of your position here as well."

"Is that so…? But tell me, do you remember that pigtailed girl—Katou, was it? Do you recall what you said to me when you shielded her and Nanami from me?"

"Oh, I remember. And I don't plan on taking back what I said, either. I'd say the same thing to everyone else gathered here, anyway."

Just like back then, we glared at each other for a brief moment until finally Minister Benito smiled.

"Well, I know now that you're not all talk."

"Hey Benito. What did he say to you?"

"Come now, it's nothing you need to worry about, Monica. You'll find out eventually. Anyway, apologies for derailing things. Go ahead," Benito said, urging President Monica to continue her point.

"If you're already aware of how things operate, I suppose I don't need to explain the Three Committees to you, do I?"

"That's right."

"Then I'll get straight to the point, okay? Join the Three Committees."

Hearing this, Minister Benito butted in with a tsk-tsk.

"Monica. I believe it's customary to speak interrogatively in moments like this, wouldn't you say? Wouldn't you agree, Saint Stefania?"

"I cannot comment on things above my station, but I'm not very fond of convention. Bad customs should be broken, I feel. Now then, Takioto. What do say to joining the Morals Committee? It may be a bit strict and rigid, but Yukine here's one of our members."

Monica looked at Saint Stef and grinned sardonically.

"I hear that of the Moral Committee members, Yukine has been especially keen on Takioto joining."

"We in the Ceremonial Committee are no different, mind you," Shion chimed in. "Salutations, Kousuke Takioto. And Nanami, too, of course. What do you say to joining the Ceremonial Committee? Either one of you would be fine by me. We'll gladly welcome you with open arms."

"Pardon me," Nanami cut in. "I have absolutely no intentions of joining any of the Three Committees. Nor do I intend to follow anyone else's orders besides my Master's. My place is standing at his side."

"Oh, is that so? So that would mean you would have to come along with Kousuke Takioto if he joined our committee, no?"

"I still won't be a part of it."

"I see. That's *quite* a titillating detail."

"…If that's settled, then why don't we get back to the topic at hand? We have something to discuss with you right now, Kousuke Takioto."

At Vice President Fran's comments, President Monica began to speak.

"Right, let's get back on topic here… To be honest, I've been interested in you from the very first instant I saw you."

Right as she said this, a cold sensation crept up and down my body.

It felt almost like the entire room was filled with static electricity, and the areas where it touched my skin felt heavy and painful. But that wasn't all. It was also cold, as if there had been a drastic temperature drop only right where I stood, causing me to shiver slightly.

This must have been a consequence of her overflowing mana. The space around Monica rippled like a heat haze, blurring her body.

"Then there was your dungeon clear a few days ago."

President Monica crossed her arms and stared at me with a sharp gleam in her eye.

She was testing me. Testing how exactly I'd react.

However, she wasn't the only one assessing me.

I felt mana and magic from Shion's direction as well, as if she was trying to add to Monica's. Pitch-black smoke manifested from Shion and gently hung in the air around her. It slowly flowed down to her feet before finally making its way toward me, ever so gingerly snaking and expanding across the floor.

Shion looked my way and squinted her eyes in glee. She must have joined in with Monica to satisfy her own curiosity.

Though the mana she was exuding wasn't as impressive as Monica's, Shion was still sending a large amount my way.

Just then, I sensed magic coming from the opposite side of the room. It looked to be coming from Yukine.

However, I got the feeling her mana wasn't being aimed in my direction. Though maybe she *had* aimed it my way. But I could sense somehow that Yukine's mana was instead wrapping around me, as if to protect me.

I felt like this was her way of reprimanding Monica and Shion. It was like she was asking, *What the hell are you both doing?*

Putting her hand on her naginata, Yukine stared down Shion with a cold look in her eye.

Shion averted her eyes from mine to meet Yukine's glare. When she did, the black smoke slowly creeping toward me pulled back, but she kept sending her mana at me.

She opened a weapon of her own, her fan, and covered her mouth. I was all but convinced that it hid a full-faced grin.

"Hee-hee, tee-hee-hee-hee-hee."

Nanami giggled at my side.

Everyone glanced at her.

"And just what is so funny, Nanami?" President Monica asked.

Nanami replied between bouts of laughter.

"This is too much. I feel like my sides are going to burst. It's hilarious that you think this amount of mana is enough to intimidate us," she said before giving a maid-like curtsey and looking in my direction. "Isn't that right, Master?"

I wanted someone to praise me for not reflexively jumping out of my skin at hearing this. Honestly, I thought she was really something else to be able to laugh at a time like this.

Seriously, what in the world was this girl doing?

Just when I thought she had taken the heat off me, she amplified everyone's expectations and made me the center of attention again. Nanami was totally laughing her ass off in that brain of hers right now, wasn't she?

Though, I didn't hate having things heat up like this, either. If anything, I suppose I should have been praising her for riling them up, huh?

Nanami had set the stage for me, so I needed to stick the landing.

"*Haaah.*"

I gave a loud, ostentatious sigh and shrugged.

Then I used enhance magic on my own body and filled my stole with as much of my mana as it could hold, readying to throw a punch at a moment's notice. A histrionic smirk twisted across my lips.

I guess it was time to give Monica an answer far beyond what she was expecting, wasn't it?

I continued sending out my mana. And more. And more still. I focused solely on transferring the entirety of my enormous mana pool into my stole, again, and again, and again, not holding anything back. Then I began scattering whatever was left into the air in an attempt to fill the entire room with mana.

There were a variety of reactions.

Vice President Fran made a bewildered expression.

Shion dispersed her mana. "*Tee-hee-hee, hah-hah-hah-hah-hah,*" she cackled.

Though she did look a bit surprised, Captain Stef kept her grip tight on her staff, ready to spring into action at a moment's notice.

Despite his smile, Minister Benito's gaze was piercing, and didn't let up his own enhance magic, either.

Yukine nodded with a sense of pride, her eyes shut.

Finally, President Monica coolly stood up and stared hard at me.

She closed her eyes and gave a small sigh. Then she slowly opened them, dispersed her mana, and fixed her gaze on me.

Seeing this, I too dispersed my mana in anticipation of her next statement.

"Fantastic. Truly fantastic...!"

She took a moment to clear her throat before continuing.

"Yukine said you have the aptitude to join any of the committees."

When I looked over at her, Yukine had her eyes shut, as if she was trying to focus her mind, but she opened one of them. After looking my way for a few brief seconds, she immediately closed it again.

▶ Chapter 3: The Three Committees

"If Yukine's endorsing him I'd say it's the truth," Vice President Fran replied, prompting a nod from President Monica.

"Very well, Kousuke Takioto. We all want you. Your drive. Your strength...... So I'll say it again. Join the Three Committees."

"That said, while there are big merits to joining the Three Committees, it comes with a fair number of drawbacks as well."

Chiming in was Minister Benito, the president of the committee with, in some sense, the biggest drawback of all.

"First, you'll need to keep secrets. You'll also need to work. You'll end up having more things to do, that's for sure. It'll be stressful, too, which might be enough to make you regret joining in the first place."

"However," Monica cut in, "I can say for certain that our Three Committees are the most optimal path for you to gain the power that you seem to be after. So take my advice. Come work for me."

"Why, pray tell, are you casually recommending he join your Student Council? Allow me to nominate the Ceremonial Committee as an option. Just take a look at me. Our committee has *quite* a bit of leeway to do as we please," Shion said before moving her hands as if they were a bird taking flight.

"The Morals Committee has the most regulations in some respects, but we have Yukine here in our ranks, you know."

Next, Captain Stef accurately highlighted the most attractive point in the Morals Committee's favor.

"You seem intent on joining the Three Committees......right?"

That went without saying. I wouldn't be able to do what I set out to do without becoming a member.

"Do you need time to think it over?"

I shook my head at the President's question.

"Then make your choice."

At Monica's decree, the vice presidents of each committee put their hands up against the insignia written on the wall.

Watching them, Saint Stefania spoke.

"Justice, and a paragon—the Morals Committee."

The Morals Committee insignia glimmered as Yukine and Saint Stefania stood in front of me.

"A paragon, and a goal—the Student Council," President Monica said before standing in front of the glimmering Student Council insignia. At her side was Vice President Fran.

"A goal, and an archenemy—the Ceremonial Committee," Minister Benito said, before lining up next to Shion in front of the Ceremonial Committee's shining insignia.

"Which one do you choose?" President Monica inquired of me, the three shining insignias at her back.

"The committee I'm going to join is…"

She didn't even need to ask me. I had acted entirely under the premise that it would be the committee I'd join.

So making the choice was no sweat. The group I was joining was of course…

"…the Ceremonial Committee."

Chapter 4 Us from Here on Out

Magical★Explorer
Reborn as a Side Character in a Fantasy Dating Sim

I was always thinking about how to make myself stronger.

What did best friend character Kousuke Takioto excel at over protagonist Iori Hijiri?

From a stats and abilities perspective, it was his mana pool. And it wasn't just Iori's mana total he surpassed; even when matched up against other high mana characters like Ludie, the Saint, and President Monica, Kousuke's pool still vastly overshadowed theirs.

Nevertheless, he expended an extremely high amount of it, too.

Most players probably took one look at his mana, which depleted even when he was idle, and avoided using him. A continuously draining mana pool was, to a certain subset of players, unbearably annoying.

That being said, his abilities were very specialized, so you could also get a lot out of him when you utilized him properly. Despite that, he still showed up in an eroge, so he was forced to be weaker than the female characters who appeared in the game.

Kousuke also had his face going for him. The heroines would probably say he was quite handsome, provided he could keep his mouth shut. His face got more compliments than Iori's plain, even cutesy, features. Just his face, though.

That about covered the in-game areas where Takioto trumped the protagonist.

He might have had a few more advantages, but they weren't really worth considering, and essentially amounted to insignificant discrepancies in stats.

On the other hand, I possessed two huge advantages over Iori Hijiri as the real-life Kousuke Takioto.

What were these two things, you ask?

Money and authority. I lived with the embodiment of power both at school and in magical academic society: Marino Hanamura. And you could never have enough influence. It was extremely useful for making things go smoothly. There was a ton of stuff I wouldn't have been able to pull off behind the scenes without Marino's help.

On top of this, I'd now gained the authority of one of the three committees, the Ceremonial Committee. Having its strength on my side would expand the range of things I could do on campus, and I'd now be able to head to a specific dungeon I had wanted to visit at any cost.

Now what about money?

Cash was another thing that you could never have too much of. In-game, almost none of the low-level and poorly equipped early game monsters would give you any trouble if you could hoard expendable items. Without the money to purchase them, my solo clear of the Tsukuyomi Dungeon, a decidedly higher-level endeavor, wouldn't have even been a consideration for me.

If I didn't have any money to my name, after I cleared the bare minimum of the dungeons I wanted to get to, I would've definitely needed to schedule time to earn some.

For what it was worth, there were many different methods of earning money in the game. So as long as you had the time, earning money wasn't much of a problem.

There were also a few downright amazing money-making methods that were used during speedruns, but they only worked if you set your morals and ethics aside. One of the most infamous had to be that event where you got your own store.

In *Magical★Explorer*, you can open an item shop of your own after triggering an event.

There, you can sell your used equipment and other items to students and adventurers and for a significant profit.

When I thought about preparing and maintaining a storefront, the benefits (i.e. money) didn't seem to outweigh the time and risk involved, so I hadn't planned on it. I did wonder if Iori would, though.

Iori had gotten some financial breathing room after subjugating those demons, but that was basically peanuts. His expenses must have been high. Weapons and armor, expendable items, and the money required to advance certain events.

And that was just what I could think of off the top of my head.

Chapter 4: Us from Here on Out

If Iori did get his own shop, I was definitely going to visit. I wanted to buy something to help him out and would even lend a hand around the store if he asked.

In that regard, I had the advantage. For some weird reason, the Hanamura house was chock-full of weapons. Plus, there was my allowance, a figure with an unbelievable amount of zeroes.

On top of that, I'd earned a considerable reward for finishing my forty-layer solo run through the Tsukuyomi Academy Dungeon.

Coupled with the points I'd earned by selling off the magic stones and item drops I had quietly amassed inside the dungeon, I'd ended up with a tremendous amount of Tsukuyomi Points.

While I would need to convert them into legal tender to use them off campus, it was a huge stack of cash, even when factoring in the exchange rate and conversion charges.

In reality, I had the profits from a luxury apartment building passively rolling in to begin with. To be honest, that alone was enough for me to live the high life.

"With all that in mind……the question is, what am I going to do from here on out?"

I had developed a few different plans under the assumption I would have both the money and authority to see them through. However, they would definitely cause deviations in future events.

The Three Committees event changes drastically depending on which you settle on, and depending on how you advance through the scenario, the characters who join the Three Committees change as well. I needed to manage some extremely difficult event flag triggers, but if I played my cards right, I'd also be allowing weird characters to join their ranks.

Even though I entered the Ceremonial Committee, I could still technically complete the events for the other committees as well. But my choice of committee would alter the details of those events, and there were still few events specific to the Morals Committee I would no longer be able to complete.

It also happened that I was the biggest unknown in these Three Committees events.

I was both self-assertive and had deviated significantly from my in-game counterpart, so a part of me was afraid that I would be locked out of certain scenes.

In which case, maybe I needed to make myself the center of each event so I could force them to happen. Otherwise, there was a chance that things would go sideways, content-wise, later down the line. Now that I was a Ceremonial Committee member, it was better for me to go all-in on their activities.

However, there was also an event that was pretty much guaranteed to pop up. It wouldn't trigger if you didn't join the Ceremonial Committee, but you were required to complete it if you did.

Knowing *her* attitude, she would lash out at me about this. She'd have a chip on her shoulder, no question about it.

She had been quiet and well-behaved up until this point. But now that grades were announced and I stood at the top of the class, I doubted she could remain that way for much longer.

I was talking about this over-the-top and haughty rich girl, whose hairstyle could be likened to drills or croissants. That character who looked strangely at home as she loudly and arrogantly chortled away.

Like Iori says in the game, she truly was—

As that thought drifted through my head, there was a quiet knock on my door. It was Ludie.

"Let's go, Kousuke."

"Right." I nodded. Today was the day Ludie and I were going out for ramen.

Despite the glaring rays of sunlight blazing down on us, it didn't actually feel that hot.

I stretched my arms up, so it looked as though the blue sky were swallowing my hands, and felt lighter immediately, like I had banished the sleepiness and fatigue from my body. I was in a strangely good mood.

The occasional breeze fluttered the beautiful golden hair of the girl merrily walking next to me, casting the smell of her usual conditioner around us.

She brushed away her bangs when the wind blew them into her eyes and sighed quietly.

"The breeze feels nice, doesn't it."

"……Yeah."

It was just about the best day for an outing you could ask for.

Ludie had been in a chipper mood ever since we left the house, but

Chapter 4: Us from Here on Out

her spirits soared even higher after we started walking beneath the clear blue sky.

The grumpy-looking cat she'd noticed stretching and sunbathing atop the gate might have also contributed to her good mood. Slightly pouty and exasperated, its expression wouldn't have been anything special on a human face. On a cat, though, it looked that much cuter. The world could be so unfair sometimes.

Speaking of unfair, Ludie had also been impossibly adorable during the encounter, smiling cheerfully and twitching her ears in time with the rhythm of the cat's tail while watching it.

Unfortunately, the soft meows that fell from her ripe, juicy lips didn't seem to get across to the cat. They did get across to *me*, however, delivering a critical hit to my heart that nearly knocked me out cold. To be honest, I wished Ludie would talk to me like that, but my reply would probably be limited to squealing pig noises, so watching by her side was for the best.

Right after we made it downtown, I glanced at the time.

"Mind if we take a bit of a detour?" I asked.

If we kept going, we were likely to hit the lunchtime rush. When I explained this to Ludie, she nodded. However, there was a problem. I had only said this to try avoiding the long line at the door, and I didn't know exactly where I wanted to go in the meantime.

Now that I thought about it, I should have read over the vague itinerary Nanami had drawn up for me.

"I was so worried about you I only slept seven hours, Master. That's why I came up with a plan of my own for you today. I'd modestly describe it as the best plan ever."

She'd handed me a piece of paper and told me this right before I left while Ludie was out of earshot.

I didn't think she needed to worry about me, but since she'd *modestly* claimed it was the best plan ever, I retorted—

"Wait, then how long's a full night sleep for you?!"

—while inwardly getting my hopes up. Despite all the buildup, when I actually looked at the plan, it just said to seduce Ludie with a sugary voice and head straight for a hotel afterward, prompting me to immediately tear it up and return it to Nanami. The fact that Nanami had written that she'd come with us to the hotel on top of all that was equally deserving of commentary.

But now that I'd considered the slim chance that the note might have contained some other useful information—despite that being as likely as a summertime snowstorm—I felt like I might've let a good thing go to waste.

"Is there somewhere you want to go, Ludie?"

"Let's see...," she replied before glancing around the area. Her gaze fell on a surprisingly mundane place—an everyday supermarket.

"Let's go there."

"Yeah, sounds good."

A supermarket? Why there?

Ludie was a daughter of nobility. While it may have been a bit judgmental, I wondered if it would normally be okay for an average guy like me to be getting so close to her, plus if she had ever been to a grocery store, like most regular people.

She apparently hadn't even visited convenience stores much before, either. In that case, it could be the same with supermarkets. Maybe she just wanted to take a look around somewhere the common folk gathered.

I thought about asking her, but......watching her make a beeline straight to the instant ramen aisle and gazing out over the selection with a solemn look on her face, I figured my thinking had missed the mark.

I stared at Ludie as she took a cup of instant ramen in each hand and carefully inspected them both.

Her long blond hair was in a half-up French braid today, so the hair that usually ran down her back was bundled together and running down her side. This allowed me to savor the beautiful, porcelain nape of her neck.

When she wore her normal, everyday clothes, she would often style her hair like this, which I though looked absolutely wonderful on her. Though with how beautiful she was, she could wear her hair however she wanted and it'd turn out fantastic.

Ludie turned to me, likely feeling my stare, and cocked her head.

"I was just thinking that hairstyle really suits you."

"Oh. Thanks."

After her slightly curt reply, she immediately turned back around, but I kept my eyes on her and saw those serious, straight lips of hers give way to a smile.

We bought our cup ramen (despite already being on our way to a ramen shop), placed the items in our item box, and left the supermarket.

Jumping off from the on-sale daikon listed on the flyer by the entrance, we began talking about pickled vegetables, animatedly chatting about our favorite salad toppings.

"Daikon is good, but cucumbers are great, too."

"Radishes and turnips aren't too shabby, either."

As we continued our conversation, we stopped by a general store that had a plushie similar to Marianne sitting in the window, and then headed to our afternoon destination.

Delaying our arrival had proven successful. There were a few people waiting in front of the shop, which was popular enough to draw a lunchtime line down the street, but it didn't seem like we'd end up waiting long.

About ten minutes later, we stepped inside.

"We have to try their most popular item first, right?!"

The top seller and most popular item here was a rich miso ramen with oodles of fat floating in the broth.

After this declaration, Ludie ordered it with a twinkle in her eye. Although she had just placed her order, she looked over the menu with a smile so bright, she seemed ready to burst into song. She was fully intent on coming here again, by the looks of it.

I ordered a plain miso ramen, purposefully trying to pick a different flavor from Ludie, and cast my eyes down at the menu she was looking at.

Ludie wasn't picky. Whether it was rich with fatback or filled with garlic, she'd slurp it all down and be ready to order an extra helping of noodles afterward. I had no doubts she'd be eating her share this time, too.

Also, whenever she visited a ramen shop, Ludie was much more talkative than usual, and today was no exception.

"So after that, right, apparently they use some special type of magic, and they're able to turn it into instant ramen without losing any flavor!"

"You've gotten real knowledgeable about ramen recently, huh……"

Ramen wasn't the only topic of conversation.

"So then, I heard Rina kicked Orange as hard as she could."

Whether talking about daily life, movies she'd seen, or books she'd read, Ludie chatted with me happily about whatever came to mind. Seeing her excitedly chatter away brought a smile to my face.

Our ramen was placed down before us a few minutes later.

"At last!" Ludie said, eyes sparkling. She adjusted her posture as if she were attending some important commemorative ceremony to face her ramen.

In the orangey-brown soup, chock-full of fat floating on the surface, was an ample serving of yellow-gray noodles. Joining them were various vegetable garnishes, a boiled egg seeped in the broth, and thick slices of *chashu* pork.

Next to it was my bowl. There wasn't as much fat floating on the surface, and the soup had more of a yellowish tinge to it. My bowl appeared to have more slices of *chashu* than hers, though.

Ludie gave her thanks and scooped up the soup in her spoon, taking a good whiff before the first sip.

"It's like I'm being assaulted with umami…"

Those were the next words out of her mouth.

I similarly scooped up some of my own soup and brought the broth, along with the green onion floating in it, into my mouth.

Since we'd ordered separate dishes, our impressions of the taste were bound to be different. I felt like the word *refined* or *elegant* best matched the flavor of my order. The spiced green onions served to enhance the broth.

After savoring a bit of the noodles, I ate a piece of *chashu*. It was extremely tender, melting inside my mouth and filling it with umami.

"The meat earns a lot of points for not being over seasoned, too."

It was fair to say the seasoning was the perfect match for the broth, which brought out the flavor of the meat.

When I said this, Ludie stared hard at my *chashu*. Conversely, I looked over at Ludie's.

Now that I'd got a good look, I noticed that thickness of her *chashu* was a little bit different. They might have adjusted the thickness and flavor to pair with the density of the overall dish. This shop had truly superb attention to detail.

I looked again at Ludie's face.

Her eyes were sparkling despite the serious expression on her face—was there anyone out there who could possibly refuse her?

"Go ahead."

She extended the hand adorned with her green ring and brought my bowl toward her. Then she sipped the soup and brought one of the pieces of *chashu* to her mouth without hesitation.

"You're right, it really does bring out the meat's umami...!"

I caught myself breaking into a smile watching her. Ludie truly ate ramen like it was the most delicious thing in the world.

Why exactly did women who ate like this, savoring every bite and flavor, look so adorable? The scene made my heart just as full as my stomach.

"*Mm*, what're you staring at me like that for? Do you want some of mine, too?"

"Okay then, just a little," I said, sipping a little of her soup before returning to my own.

After that, I finished eating all of my noodles. Ludie spoke up as I started thinking about what I was going to do with the leftover broth.

"Oh right. You might already know Kousuke, but...I got an invitation from Yukine yesterday morning."

"Right." I nodded.

"I......I'm thinking about joining the Morals Committee."

"I think that's a good idea."

On a personal level, I agreed with Ludie joining the Three Committees. But considering her position as an imperial princess, I didn't think the Ceremonial Committee was a good idea. On the Student Council or the Morals Committee, however, her status as an imperial princess wouldn't shackle her. Both groups would boost her reputation after graduation as well.

"It was a personal invitation from Yukine, so she said it still needs to go through Saint Scaglione, though."

"Nah, you'll be fine. There's no reason not to accept, and the Saint's not gonna turn you down."

"And how can you be so sure?"

Because the Saint probably didn't give a damn either way. Naturally, I wasn't going to tell Ludie that, though.

"Personally, I feel like their decision is obvious—they'd be foolish to reject you. Objectively speaking, anyone would think you should join."

Ludie's grades were superb, she was extremely popular, and she was skilled in combat. Both subjectively and objectively, she was nothing but the perfect candidate.

"I know you, Ludie. I would've tried to convince you to join the Ceremonial Committee, but I think you'd be a perfect fit for both the Student Council and the Morals Committee. Especially if you want to develop yourself even further. I'd cheer you on either way. Though, I guess it'd be better to say we'd both be working hard together, really."

"Right, that's just it."

Ludie moved her ramen bowl, finishing one step ahead of me, to make it easier for the waitstaff to pick it up.

"What exactly do the Three Committees do, anyway?"

I gathered that she probably wasn't asking about what the public thought they did.

I looked around and sighed.

"...Let's go somewhere else to talk."

"Here, please relax and take your time."

A women dressed in hemp leaf–patterned clothes said this to us, then bowed and left. Ludie and I were the only customers inside the Japanese-style room we had been seated in.

I watched as Ludie dug into the matcha cheesecake in front of her, a huge smile on her face, before asking my question.

"Before I get into things, just how much do you know about the Three Committees already, Ludie?"

"The Student Council runs the School Festival and the Tsukuyomi Tournament and stuff, right? The Morals Committee does just what their name says and enforces discipline."

I nodded.

"And the group I joined, the Ceremonial Committee, does audits and personnel stuff, along with a buncha behind-the-scenes matters, too," I informed her.

Well, these were all the widely known facts that everyone could check in their Tsukuyomi Traveler, right next to the school rules and regulations. But that wasn't all.

"Now, you might've picked up on it already, but the Three Committees have duties beyond that."

"I guessed as much, though I wasn't one hundred percent positive. Seeing you join the Ceremonial Committee really convinced me. I imagine anyone that doesn't really know you probably feels a little confused by the news, wouldn't you say?

"Like Iori or Rina," Ludie added.

She had a point that those two might find it unusual. Iori was already considered a leading student within one of the Student Council's sub-organizations, anyway, so he'd probably learn about certain things sooner rather than later.

"You're right. They have hidden duties they carry out behind the scenes."

"I knew it……"

"And, as for what those roles *are*…… Hrm. I guess I'll talk about the themes first. Each of the Three Committees has thematic keywords that represent their hidden roles. The words for the Morals Committee are 'justice' and 'paragon.' The Student Council's are 'paragon' and 'goal.' And the Ceremonial Committee's are 'goal' and 'archenemy.'"

"A few of the keywords seem to overlap, then?"

"Right. Each of the Three Committees has their own different themes, but in truth, they all work to achieve a single goal."

"Just one?"

"Yup, to develop the abilities of the Academy students."

"……That's a bit ordinary, isn't it?"

"Oh yeah, of course it's ordinary. But when you consider what the Academy is for, it's really important, right?"

Some students became researchers after graduating, while others joined the Knight Corps. Several became adventurers who set out for the new world, and others became explorers who cleared dungeons. What these students sought above all else were the abilities they needed to pursue their goals, and the Magic Academy was there to help foster them.

"Fair enough."

"Why don't I explain each of the committees? Let's start with the Morals Committee…… Though, I guess Yukine'll fill in the details for you anyway, so I'll keep it simple. The 'paragon' theme is just what the word implies; it means committing yourself to setting a proper example that the other students can look to. Meanwhile for 'justice,' well, I'm sure you can guess what that's about, since they oversee the Academy discipline and such. However, they have one other role, too… You'll have to ask Yukine to fill you in on the details there."

"Ask her...? Fine."

I paused for a moment and took a bite of my matcha parfait.

"Now, I guess the Student Council's next... But before that, I should throw in a presupposition."

"A presupposition?"

"Yeah, to make this easier to understand...... Okay. What do you think is necessary for the students' abilities to develop and improve?"

"That's quite a vague question. Let's see... Studying, training. And going into the dungeon, I suppose?"

"Yeah, that's fair. There's one more thing, though."

I nodded as I brought a spoonful of parfait to my mouth. Then, pulling the spoon back out, I thrust it into the ice cream like I was swinging a sword.

"Quality's also a factor with training and learning."

"Quality?"

"Well, there's good training and there's bad training, and that determines just how beneficial it'll end up being for you."

"I guess I get what you're trying to say," Ludie said, putting her fork down on her plate. "In other words, you're saying that you can get better training than normal if you have a good teacher to guide you in an effective environment, right?"

"Yeah, exactly. The roles of the Student Council and the Ceremonial Committee are linked to improving that level of quality."

"What do you mean?"

"The Student Council and Ceremonial Committee shoulder the role of encouraging the students toward beneficial forms of learning, basically. They're responsible for a critical element that has a whole bunch of wide-reaching effects: motivation."

Some students grow with praise, others improve by getting yelled at. Similarly, while some kids get more motivated by having goals or friends joining them, there were others who got more motivated by having a rival serve as their model.

"Take this, for example. If you saw an upperclassman you love and respect diligently studying in the library, it'd make you want to do your best and study harder, too, right? Or if there was some dude you hated who was always goofing around and slacking off in class, you might think, 'I can't let myself lose to a jerk like him!' wouldn't you?"

"I would...... I get it."

"Anyway, the Student Council's themes are 'paragon' and 'goal.' They exist to become an objective the students can strive toward and to motivate them to do so. They also have a duty to occasionally stand on the student's side and encourage them directly by praising them, comforting them, etcetera."

"Right. So if the Student Council is a 'goal to aspire to,' and the Ceremonial Committee is an 'archenemy' and 'goal'…… They're basically people to defeat, then."

"Yup, you've pretty much guessed it. The Ceremonial Committee's keywords are 'archenemy' and 'objective.' They purposefully play the role of campus bad guy to earn the ire of the student body, becoming somebody their classmates will get fired up about taking down."

"I suspected they weren't truly evil since you decided to join them, but I guess it turns out they purposefully play the villain."

To be honest, the system really only worked because this was a video game world. It would never go that smoothly in real life, and it probably wouldn't even be possible to implement to begin with.

"And that's not all. By acting as the students' common enemy, the Ceremonial Committee fulfills yet another duty. Probably the most important of all, as far as the Morals Committee and the Academy as a whole are concerned."

"Another duty?"

"Yup, they unite the student body together, and improve the overall peace and security of the school."

"How do they do that?"

"Forming a shared goal is an okay way of promoting collective unity, but making a shared *enemy* is overwhelmingly more effective. People are easier to unite when they all hate something, or they're all jealous of something. And…"

"And what…?"

"You've heard the phrase 'the enemy of my enemy is my friend,' right? By single-handedly taking on the brunt of everyone's negative emotions, the Ceremonial Committee stops students from aiming their negative feelings anywhere else."

Though this *could* backfire sometimes, which called for another special way of handling things.

Ludie narrowed her eyes slightly.

"Doesn't that make the Ceremonial Committee pretty dangerous…?"

"That's all the more reason why there are special conditions to join the Ceremonial Committee. You need overwhelming fighting strength or authority outside of school to keep people in line."

Ludie seemed convinced, nodding before she cut her cheesecake with her fork.

"You're both a member of the Hanamura family and capable of soloing forty layers of the Academy Dungeon… I can't really see anyone trying to mess with you, that's for sure. But that won't be enough to protect you completely, right? It sounds like you'll still be challenged to duels and whatnot, no?"

"I'm sure it'll happen eventually."

I could imagine the trouble that'd kick up once news that I joined was made public. I needed to finish getting my classmates all on the same page before that happened.

"That said, upperclassmen are forbidden from challenging first-years to a duel for a little while, so it'll only be first-years challenging me, anyway. Not much time's gone by since we started school, so I doubt there'll be anyone who'd challenge… *Oh.*"

"…Well, that certainly sounded ominous."

"N-nah. I'll be fine. Probably. Besides, if push comes to shove, I'd win the duel anyway."

I had forgotten about the haughty, drill-haired rich girl. I felt…… slightly uneasy thinking about her. W-well, that was a problem for future Takioto.

"Do you realize how tense you look right now…?"

"No, I'm fine. Yup, gonna be totally fine. There, I've convinced myself into believing it'll work out, no problem. Let's get back on topic. We were talking about the Ceremonial Committee, right?"

"You're definitely not okay… You better tell me if something happens."

"Thanks. I'm leaving it in your hands, then."

Except when it came to *her*, I didn't think I'd be able to count on Ludie for much.

"So basically, the Ceremonial Committee has a bit of a unique role to play. People will hate me. I might even get jumped or something a few times. That's why there's a committee that's tasked with secretly protecting us from any harm."

"I know. The Morals Committee, right?"

"Yup, pretty much. On the surface, the Morals Committee and the Ceremonial Committee are perceived as being almost at odds with each other, but in reality, they work closely together. In order to focus all the student's hate at one group, the Three Committees, Student Council included, act out their parts in public. But once they're done, they all go back to celebrate a job well done together."

"Then, does that mean that first time we saw the Three Committees feuding…"

She must have been referring to back when I'd been explaining everything to Iori and the others. Naturally—

"That was all an act, of course."

Ludie breathed a small sigh.

"Just hearing that makes me think that the 'justice' the Morals Committee talks about isn't really just at all."

……*That's fair*, I thought.

"Anyway, that's the long and short of it. There's still more stuff they do in addition to that, but let's leave things at that for now."

She seemed to have understood the broad outline of it all. Of course, there were still the rivalries and other things that happened behind the scenes, too, as well as the Three Committee's true purpose. Maybe it would be a good idea to clear down to layer sixty so I could get the committee presidents to explain their true purpose to me ASAP.

"Are you going to start doing Ceremonial Committee work soon?"

"Yeah. They said they're throwing me a welcome party for now. The Morals Committee'll probably do the same for you, too."

In the game, there's a welcome party no matter which committee you join.

"You think so?"

"Yeah, Yukine will throw you one for sure. Okay, time for me to seriously dig into this parfait," I said before scooping up some of the matcha ice cream and taking a bite. Shortly after, having finished her matcha cheesecake, Ludie quietly murmured:

"Eating something sweet like this gives me a hankering for ramen… Hey! I'm not going *now*, I'm too full, obviously. Don't give me that look."

Chapter 5 — Bienvenue, Ceremonial Committee

"Yaaaaaaaaay! Wooohooooo! Welcome to the Ceremonial Committee!"

"Th-thank you."

I thanked the rabbit-eared upperclassman who had set off the party popper. After tossing the used popper into the trash can, she immediately exchanged it for a glass. Then, placing her hand on my shoulder, she raised it up to the ceiling.

"Congratulations! I *knew* you would join one of the Three Committees, but I'm so glad you joined ours. Yaaaaaaaaaaaaay!" she said, her eyes practically forming sideways triangles as she thrust a cocktail glass up against my cheek. While this was no different from how she acted in-game, her hyperactive energy left me stunned.

Suddenly noticing the pressure from her was gone, I turned to find that Nanami had grabbed the girl by the scruff of her neck and lifted her into the air.

"Awwww, you caught meee! Wooohoooooooooo!"

She continued gulping down the Blue Hawaii–colored liquid in her glass even as she dangled in the air.

"Is she drunk, perhaps?"

Nanami must've assumed as much from the fact that she was holding a cocktail glass. However.

"No, her brain is simply bubbling with energy twenty-four seven, I'm afraid."

I got where she was coming from, but that still felt like a bit of a mean way to put it.

"Whoa, whoa, c'mon Shishi! Why do you gotta treat me like that!"

"Could you stow that nickname of yours while you're at it?" Shion said, heaving a sigh. Minister Benito laughed as he watched this all unfold.

"*Hah-hah-hah*, well, that's what's great about her, right? All right, why don't we briefly introduce ourselves to the new member?"

He put a hand on his chest and smiled.

"I'm Ceremonial Minister Benito Evangelista. Things might get a bit confusing with my little sister around, so feel free to call me Benito."

He finished with a wink. It perfectly complemented his dashing good looks.

"Vice Minister Shion Himemiya. You may call me Shion. Welcome aboard," Shion said, giving me a handshake, which then prompted the rabbit-eared upperclassman to exclaim, "My turn, my turn!" She had apparently managed to escape Nanami's grasp at some point.

"I'm editor-in-chief and president of the school newspaper, as well as Tsukuyomi Magic Academy's idol, Ivy! Just Ivy's fine, but make sure you say it with love, okay?"

"I'm Kousuke Takioto, and this is—"

"His stunningly beautiful maid Nanami. Just Nanami or Nanamin is fine with me," she said, letting go of Ivy and curtseying.

The loss of support set Ivy flopping on the ground, and she complained in pain as she rubbed her butt, which had a soft fluffy tail. Sheesh, how I wished I could be its chair.

"Glad you found your way here. And sorry about the hastily put together welcome party."

"Oh, not at all. I'm thrilled that you would throw a party on my behalf at all."

"Come now, what is that stuffy nonsense all about, then?" Shion said, placing her hand on my shoulder.

"But Vice Minister Himemiya, you and everyone else here are upperclassmen, so…"

"And we're in the same committee now, aren't we? Lighten up. Just Shion is fine with me."

Minister Benito also nodded along at Shion's statement.

"She's right. There's no need to get all stuffy and formal here in the Ceremonial Committee!"

"Though there *are* some stuffier associates of ours in the Morals Committee and Student Council, so do take care when talking to them, you hear?"

▶ Chapter 5: Bienvenue, Ceremonial Committee

I nodded. Then Nanami chimed in.

"Speaking of which, where are the other members? I had heard that the Ceremonial Committee had two members from each grade."

Responding to her question, Shion shook her head, looking embarrassed.

"Ah, yes. They couldn't make it, unfortunately. One of them was absolutely dying to come, but something came up they simply had to attend to."

"And what about the other person?"

I already knew why they weren't here, but I figured I should ask this to keep the conversation moving.

"Ah, yes, well, they are in my year, but they usually don't show up. They didn't even read my message at all. Feel free to think of them as a shut-in."

"We'll introduce both of them to you later. Also, I imagine you have one other question about the members we've gathered here..."

Everyone's gaze fell on Ivy.

"Whoopsie, you got me!"

"I saw you confront the school newspaper a while back, Benito. Following that incident I heard that......succinctly put, the articles were filled top to bottom with indirect insults and abuse lobbied at you."

"Aww shucks, it's a little embarrassing to hear you saw all of that! Clinched my best actress nom, for sure!"

"She's really hyper, huh."

"Always keeps our spirits up, that's for sure. Okay, let me explain everything in order here. I'm sure you already know, but the Student Council and the Morals Committee have organizations that assist them. The Class Representative Assembly requires a member from each class. However, there are cases where several people are recommended by the Student Council or the teachers for the position. Those individuals all become nominees for the Student Council."

This was where Iori currently stood. He was a Student Council nominee who joined the Class Representative Assembly under the President's recommendation. In a beginner's first playthrough of the game, I imagined this would be their route into joining the Three Committees.

"The Morals Committee has the Lifestyle Beautification Assembly.

Almost everyone needs a recommendation to join them, but in turn, all of their members are Morals Committee nominees."

"I guess both the Student Council and the Morals Committee want to recruit anyone they see with potential. Though, there are a lot of incredible students this year, so they might just skip over that and be added directly. It's happened before. In an average year, first-years slowly climb through the ranks, but it seems like there'll be more students who jump straight into the Committees than not this year," he said, looking at me.

"I see, that clears up a lot. Then what about Ivy here?" Nanami asked, prompting a nod from Minister Benito.

"She's an unofficial Ceremonial Committee nominee. Basically..."

"The school newspaper hurls all manner of nastiness our way, but the truth is, they've got a deep, *deep* relationship with the Ceremonial Committee," Shion said before draining the rest of the clear vermilion liquid in her glass.

"Which means I also know aaaaaall about the roles of the Three Committees, too! That confrontation before was totally, completely, one hundred and ten percent on purpose. A big fat phony sham!" Ivy said, beaming.

"That said, there are still some members of the school newspaper who don't know about the Three Committees' duties, so we have to be careful about what info gets out."

"And that's why we got the members we did together today."

"I see. Thank you for the explanation."

"Now as much as I would love to dig into the fruits our Minister here has provided...I thought we might go over the workload here in our committee."

"Right, right. Takioto. Brace yourself for what I'm going to tell you. Actually, here at the Ceremonial Committee...," Benito said, looking dead serious. Beside me, Shion wore a solemn look, as if there was a deeply troubling problem at hand. Finally, even Ivy had folded her ears down and lowered her eyes to the ground.

Amid it all, Benito inhaled deeply for a moment before continuing.

"The truth is......we basically don't do anything at all!"

His expression immediately dissolved into laughter at the startling revelation. Sitting beside him, Shion, too, burst out into a cackle.

"As for the 'auditing' we're supposed to be doing, the Student Council has that covered. They're perfectionists."

"Fran's a bit stubborn, but she's quite a diligent worker, indeed. We just sign whatever she asks us to and hand it back to her."

"That's why sometimes I suspect the newspaper is actually the busier of our two divisions. Thaaaat's the reality!"

"Yup, and the secret work's pretty straightforward, too."

"It is?"

"The funny thing with people is that you only need to do something truly heinous to them once for anything you do after that to enrage them."

"Quite so. Why, the hatred sinks into their hearts like an anchor! *Hah-hah-hah!*"

"Once it gets to that point, they're never going to have a good impression of us, unless something really wild happens. With our goals accomplished, we're just free to do whatever!"

"We will go rile up the students occasionally, of course."

"Causing some sort of commotion and getting the paper to cover it is usually enough to fulfill our duties."

"Well, if that'll get them motivated, then I'll whip them into as much of a frenzy as necessary. Oh, right, Takioto. I'm guessing this is unnecessary concern on my part, but there's something I need to tell you."

"What would that be?"

Nodding in affirmation, Minister Benito continued, "The hostile looks you're going to get from here on out will be much worse than you've endured up until now."

"Even worse?"

"Yes, that's right. Between your appearance, the friends you have with you, and your abilities, you already have a ton of attention on you. I gather you've been hit with plenty of negative sentiments from the other students."

Well, I had gotten those stares back during all the stuff with Ludie. Not that it had bothered me much.

"It's possible you're going to be exposed to a level of hostility unlike anything yet."

"The Ceremonial Committee was active before we joined it, mind you. Thanks to that, it's been building up ill-will with the students for a long, and I do mean *loooong* time."

"That's precisely why we're their 'archenemy.' Only people capable of enduring their resentment are allowed to join our ranks."

"The Ceremonial Committee doesn't let its members quit; if people start to think of us as cowards, why, all that built-up malice will go up in smoke, now, won't it?"

"I'll be fine. I'm looking forward to playing my part with all of you."

"Oh my, oh my! Now, what do you say, Nanami? Want to officially join us?"

"I'm extremely honored by your invitation, but I do not intend on giving myself any more work beyond my serving as Master's maid."

Nanami seemed intent on staying out of the Ceremonial Committee no matter what. Though, she would still accompany me while I worked for the committee, so she was pretty much a member for all intents and purposes.

"Are you sure that's okay? For Nanami to be here with me anyway?"

"Yeah, we don't mind. She's got that card of hers, after all. In some respects, that gives her more power than me, the ceremonial minister."

Normally Nanami would have showed off the card to me while barely holding back a smug chuckle, but today we weren't in the company of Yukine or Ludie, but rather Minister Benito, Shion, and Ivy.

Nevertheless, she still had a smirk of delight on her face.

Why had Marino made her carry that anyway...? Knowing Marino, she probably gave it to Nanami so she could look after me, but...she was surprisingly overprotective. Thanks to that, though, I was eternally in her debt.

"I mean, for starters? The Ceremonial Committee is unique in several ways that differ from the Student Council and the Morals Committee. No one would bat an eyelash if we had an exclusive maid or two with us."

"If anything, it might prove useful for offending the students. Though I feel like that's been happening already."

"Pretty much." I nodded.

Since Nanami had been aware of my objectives before I joined the committee, she'd been intentionally attracting the ire of other students.

Granted, I was pretty sure she was mainly doing it because she found their reactions entertaining.

"What do you want to do about your induction announcement? Want to put it up tomorrow? Is that okay?"

"Yeah, that's fine by me."

I had already gotten my classmates up to speed. Or rather, Iori had. I would be okay even after becoming Kousuke Takioto, member of the Ceremonial Committee. Probably.

"Well then, best to put it up on the bulletin board, yes?"

"Yeah... Might be good to stir up the students with it, too."

"You can leave Taky to me★! I'll write up eeeeeeeeeeeeverything—facts, fiction, and everything in between! Just watch!"

Who the hell was Taky?

"The info already out there should be plenty for Takioto... By the way, were you purposefully keeping quiet about being a member of the Hanamura family?"

"I wasn't doing it on purpose, really... No one ever asked, so I never mentioned it."

"I see," Minister Benito murmured. He closed his eyes, mulling over something with his arms crossed, before opening an eye after a few moments and smiling.

"In that case, you don't mind us announcing that to everyone, do you? Since it seems like there's a lot fewer people who know you're a Hanamura than you think there are."

"Sure, I don't mind."

"*Tee-hee-hee*. Oh yes, I'm drooling just thinking of the article already!"

Although I had been keeping my lineage on the down-low, I hadn't really concealed the fact, either. Apparently, it was less well known than I thought.

"I'd like to make this fact public as naturally as possible. Think you can handle it, Ivy?"

"You got it, boss! Right, right. I'll write up an article later, so I'll need Taky and Nanamin's help, too."

"Okay. I can do that."

"All that aside, it feels like I'm doing real Ceremonial Committee work for the first time in a while! *Hah-hah-hah*!"

"Indeed. We haven't done much public activity lately, have we? Though we have been dropping by on the sly to assist the other two committees. Speaking of which, that forty-layer dungeon romp of yours appeared to have given the Student Council and Morals Committee a rather fantastic headache."

"Yeah, I apologized to Yukine..."

"Oh please, you certainly don't need to apologize to her. Why, she was so enthusiastic about your escapades, I swear she seemed ready to handle all that work and more if it meant helping you out. The Saint did seem annoyed by it, but honestly, when isn't she?"

"Hah-hah-hah."

I decided to laugh it off.

Shion appeared to suddenly recall something and clapped her hands together.

"Ah, yes, yes. That does remind me—it appears the Morals Committee will be gaining a new member as well. And a significant one at that."

"Right, Ludie's joining. I already heard so from Yukine and herself."

"Oh really...?" Minister Benito murmured, grinning.

"Pray tell, what prompted that smirk, Minister?"

"Nothing really. I just had a thought. I had my suspicions after Lieutenant Mizumori made that declaration of hers, but I'd say they're all but confirmed now...... *Hee-hee.*"

"...Now you're just being creepy. What in the world are you on about?"

"I guess it'd be better to keep it a secret for now, right Takioto?"

"Keep what a secret?"

"Actually, there's something I want to ask you."

"Really?"

"There sure is. It's fine if you don't have an answer. Who among the first-years is talented and skilled enough to join the Three Committees?"

Hmmm. I pondered. There were several names I could bring up to answer the question.

When it came to just fighting skills, Katorina would work. Once you factored in personality, the Class Rep fit the bill, as well as Yuika, with her abilities and her wiles. The same went for that beastfolk kid, or Benito's younger sister, too. All that being said—

"There's actually a fair number of students to keep an eye on, but there's one that stands out even further from the pack."

Chapter 5: Bienvenue, Ceremonial Committee

There was only person who was a true standout.

"Really now? You think we could scout them for the newspaper then?"

"Unfortunately, someone's already claimed him for their own. Ivy's probably directly met with him, too."

His demon-vanquishing feats had even gotten a feature in the Tsukuyomi Academy Paper, after all.

"Both you, Minister Benito, and Shion as well, should remember this name. Just looking at his potentiality, he could stand shoulder to shoulder with President Monica."

He wouldn't lose to the others in the Big Three, Yukine and the Founding Saint, either.

"...You're saying there's another monster among those classmates of yours besides you?"

"Woooooow! Are they, like, human?"

"Now you've piqued my interest."

Wait, so I was a monster now?

"Yeah, he's definitely going to shoot up the ranks. He might not stand out too much at the moment, but I bet he's going to earn a reputation for himself from here on out."

"Why, I am on the edge of my seat here... Just who is this wunderkind?"

"The Student Council has known about him from the start, but the Ceremonial Committee should've heard his name mentioned before, too."

Whether it was melee combat, long-ranged magic, the skills he could learn, or his growth potential, he was given preferential treatment with all of it—he was the protagonist of Magical★Explorer.

"His name is Iori Hijiri."

—*Ludie's Perspective*—

The Morals Committee's formal initiation ceremony wrapped up after afternoon classes had finished and the students were on their way home.

"Sorry about putting you through all of that, Ludie. I bet a lot of it must've come as a real surprise."

"Kousuke had told me a bit about it beforehand, but... Even then, it was still a shock."

It had all been exactly as Kousuke had said. The Three Committees I had thought were all opposed to one another were internally on peaceful and friendly terms. On top of that, the group that made the most enemies and earned the most hate, the Ceremonial Committee, was actually the heart and soul of the Three Committees.

Passing by students heading back to their dorm rooms, Yukine gave a small sigh.

"This year's new students are a handful."

"They are?"

"A big one, too. Haven't you heard…? There's a guy in our year that cleared forty layers of the school dungeon solo, then immediately joined the Three Committees."

I couldn't hold back a dry chuckle.

"I suppose you're right."

"*Tee-hee*," Yukine laughed as well. "It feels like we've been hit by a typhoon and the storm's not going anywhere." Then she added, "He's going to get up to more trouble, too, I bet," but she didn't look bothered by it at all.

"Thanks to all that, the first-years have a totally different vibe than they did last year. He joined the Ceremonial Committee, too, so he's going to be constantly at the center of attention from here on out."

Indeed, the eyes of every student in the Academy would be on him. In the worst way possible.

The boy who everyone had considered beneath them, who they had secretly all made fun of, the boy who had basically ditched his classes and barely came to campus, had managed to pull off something beyond what not only the first-years but also the upperclassmen were capable of.

And while he had bared his feelings to us about how hard the experience was, it didn't help that he came across as a superficial jokester to anyone he wasn't close with.

I figured that was why the people he didn't know saw him as a "strange but super powerful guy." His solo conquest of forty dungeon layers had made everyone reevaluate him.

However, his decision to join the Ceremonial Committee would negate everyone's slightly improved impression of him and only make him even more hated.

Chapter 5: Bienvenue, Ceremonial Committee

Nevertheless, Kousuke didn't seem bothered by any of it this time, either. That I could say with confidence.

The same had been true when I was the root of the problem. I had thought that Kousuke would have regarded the students' gossip and slander as an ill wind buffeting against him. The kind that would normally make someone stumble and prevent them from moving forward before they took shelter somewhere or blew backward entirely.

But Kousuke was different.

He wasn't concerned at all with where or how such a wind blew. After Nanami arrived, he'd even seemed to revel in the reactions of the other students.

If anything, he appeared to be using that ill wind to spread his wings and fly like a bird to even greater heights.

No, that wasn't it—Kousuke was already flapping his wings wide. He'd even given us wings of our own: the wings of potential.

"Kousuke……really is incredible. I need to give it my all, too."

"…If you ask me, you're incredible yourself, Ludie."

"I am?"

"Comparing yourself to Takioto probably makes it harder to realize, but…… You joined the Three Committees, too, you know," Yukine said before looking down at her Tsukuyomi Traveler.

"It's time. Let's go check the bulletin board. It should be officially announced any moment now."

I nodded, and we started heading in the direction of the bulletin board.

In front of the display were a number of students who had stopped on their way home to look up at the screen.

Nearby, three female students widened their eyes and stared vacantly up at the bulletin board, mouths agape. From the brooch that was pinned to their uniform, they looked to be third-years.

One of the girls muttered something.

"No way…"

"…I've never heard of them appointing someone this time of year."

They whispered to each other, still gazing up at the bulletin board.

I turned my attention from them to the bulletin board as well. They would probably announce my own induction in a similar way.

NEWS BOARD

The following student has been appointed as Assistant Vice Minister, one of the Ceremonial Committee's Vice Presidential positions.

First Year
Kousuke Takioto

Ceremonial Committee
Ceremonial Minister
Benito Evangelista

"Wh-whoa, hold up!"

Suddenly, one of the girls shouted in surprise. She had her Tsukuyomi Traveler in her hand and was shaking one of the other girls by the shoulders in a fluster.

"Quick, check your Tsukuyomi Traveler."

"What? It's just going to be more about the Ceremonial Committee, right?"

"Yeah, it is, but that's not it... Takioto......he's part of *the* Hanamura family."

Listening to their conversation, I took out my own Tsukuyomi Traveler and opened the new breaking news report.

Yukine peeked over from beside me to look at my screen.

Tsukuyomi Breaking News

Breaking News!

Ceremonial Committee Minister Benito Evangelista has appointed first-year Kousuke Takioto to the role of Assistant Vice-Minister.

The great-grandson of Ryuuen Hanamura and second cousin of Ms. Hatsumi Hanamura, Kousuke Takioto set a record the other day with his one-week solo conquest of the first forty floors of the Tsukuyomi Academy Dungeon. It is believed that his appointment came in light of this unprecedented achievement.

We at the Tsukuyomi Academy Newspaper plan to interview Kousuke Takioto in the near future. For those of you interested, please look forward to our upcoming issues!

Tsukuyomi Academy Newspaper

Chapter 6: A Dangerous Machine

I parted ways with the other members of the Ceremonial Committee after their announcement went live, returned home, and finished dinner. Then it happened.

Nanami asked everyone to move into the living room.

Waiting there for us was not the normal living room table, but instead something covered in a sheet of cloth. Sis, Ludie, Claris, and Yukine were all staring at the strange new item.

"Whatever could it be?" Ludie asked me as I walked up next to her. When I turned to look at the others, it seemed neither Claris nor Yukine had any clue what they were looking at. Sis remained expressionless.

"It seems your interest has been piqued. This is a fantastic item for your training. I set it up in the hopes everyone would get some benefits from it," Nanami announced, taking a peek at the cloth-covered item. Then she muttered some nonsense about it "being worth the hard work of limiting myself to three meals a day" as she pretended to use her apron to wipe away her tears.

"That just makes me wonder how many meals you usually eat in a day."

Three was pretty much the standard number of meals wherever you went.

But about this mysterious something in front of Nanami... I couldn't tell what it was with that cloth draped over it, but the object seemed to be a little bit smaller than the average adult man. It was about as long as one, too.

"Well, what is this thing, then?"

"It is, in fact, an exercise machine," Nanami said, instantly returning to normal despite her previous fake crying routine.

"What for?"

"To assist with your training regimen. I believe you can use this whenever there's a downpour, typhoon, blizzard, or 'tsunanami.'"

"You really inserted yourself into those natural weather patterns quite naturally, huh."

Besides, she just slipped an extra *na* into *tsunami*. What the hell was a "tsunanami" even supposed to be?

"Come now, Master, it's that thing that comes seven times a week."

"You know, hearing that it comes every day makes me even more confused!"

All that did was give me more questions! Actually, why had she used such a difficult to parse phrase like "seven times a week," to explain it in the first place?

"Now, please relish and savor my gift to you. *Drundrundrundrundruuuuun—*"

"Savor? You can't eat it, c'mon."

"*Dorun!* A r—*uuuuuhn* ♪!—ning machiiiiiiiiiine!" Nanami said before taking off the sheet covering the device. But what was up with the cry of ecstasy in the middle there?

"This will let you run whenever you want, Master."

"Really? I'm impressed you were able to put something like this together."

"Yes, well, I bought the item at a heavily discounted price from a sketchy antique shop of sorts and remodeled it using my own personal theories to figure out the parts that I didn't really understand."

"I get the sense there's a lot of concerning elements to that story, but I'm just overthinking things, right?"

An antique shop of sorts, was it? Part of me felt like I knew exactly where she might've gone, but maybe I was wrong.

While I was lost in thought, Nanami touched the unveiled machine.

"Since you're here already, would you like to test it out? It is very easy to use."

"Is it now? I've got alarm bells ringing like a jet engine in my head right now, but I guess I could give it a spin."

"It's setting off alarms and you're *still* going to try it…?"

I gave Ludie a strained smile as she exasperatedly made it clear I wouldn't get any pity from her if things went south. This thing couldn't have deviated that far from its treadmill origins. That's what I figured.

Chapter 6: A Dangerous Machine

"Now that you've steeled yourself, Master, go ahead and press the power button first."

I pressed the button that featured the same circle with a line through it found on any computer. When I did, an image appeared in the air before my eyes. It was of a human body, along with a number of different meters.

"Normally, you would register yourself with the treadmill, but I registered it with myself ahead of time."

"Oh wow, there's a user registration?"

"It stores various pieces of information, such as your name, sex, birthday, favorite maid, height, and your body measurements. I already made sure to put myself down for the favorite maid question."

"Why does it know my measurements so minutely down to a fraction of a centimeter? And my favorite maid? Yeah, that's *definitely* not something you need to sign up for a gym."

"By registering yourself with the machine, you can utilize a wide range of functions, including your daily usage history, your average running distance, and the calories you've burned."

"Figured you'd just cruise right past that little detail. Anyways, it seems pretty convenient."

"It can scan you during user registration to measure your weight and height as well. It can also obtain data on your body fat percentage, your daily calorie expenditure, and send all the data to your Tsukuyomi Traveler."

"An impressive set of functions. Makes me want to try it out myself."

It appeared Yukine was also interested in the machine. While it didn't show on her face, Claris seemed intrigued, too.

"Rest assured, I've registered everyone in the house besides Marino in the machine already. However, I'll need everyone besides Master to set their main maid or butler."

"And what the hell's a 'main maid' supposed to be?"

"Naturally, your main maid is myself, Master."

"That really doesn't answer my question."

I guess Nanami was the only thing that came to mind when I heard the word *maid*, anyway.

"Additionally, you are able to change your main maid. While most people can change their settings easily, out of consideration for your security, I've protected your details and yours alone behind seventy-three layers of authentication."

"Just how much security does a guy need?!"

"I plan on submitting a patent application for my Nanami Security System."

"I doubt anyone will ever user it, so don't bother. Getting back to the important question, though, what the heck's a main maid?"

"A main maid or butler is the person who assists the user on their run. The details of said assistance should become clear as you operate the machine."

In that case, I supposed I'd go ahead and give it a try.

<Please make your selection via the touch panel or voice commands.>

"Whoa, it spoke. Oh, I get it, so it's like a computer assistant kind of deal. That was your voice, but I'm assuming it'll change depending on the main maid selection, then?"

"That's right."

"Huh. That actually seems like it'll be useful."

I had to hand it to Nanami that using voice commands to operate the machine was definitely convenient.

"First, let's set a goal. The default is set to be a distance of forty-two kilometers."

"Way too long, as always."

"Your Big Sis can't run. No running for Big Sis. Nope, not for Big Sis."

Sis *reeeeally* wanted me to call her Big Sis again, huh.

"You think so? I think it's about the perfect distance myself. Don't you agree, Claris?"

"*Hah-hah-hah...* I think it's perfectly suited to you and Takioto, that's for sure."

"You'll be able to adjust your distance goals later, of course."

That was a pretty fundamental function to have, yes.

"Furthermore, if you meet your distance goal, or have a particularly fantastic run, the main maid's voice—by which I mean my voice—will praise you depending on how far you ran."

"I did think it was a little bit strange that when I did my practice swings in the garden, I saw Nanami calling out in this alluring voice into a microphone."

Chapter 6: A Dangerous Machine

Wouldn't that have been a good time to comment on her ridiculousness, Yukine? Though, with Nanami, you'd be there all day if you tried to come up with a quip for everything she did.

"Rest assured that I've also equipped it with a system that will allow you to swap the voice and image with that of either Master, Miss Ludie, Miss Claris, Miss Yukine, or Miss Hatsumi," Nanami said before touching the image floating in front of her. This displayed the main maid header, along with a picture of Nanami's face below it. When she touched her face, it then displayed the faces of Ludie, Yukine, Claris, Sis, and for some reason, myself as well. Seriously, why was I included in here, too?

"Hold on, Nanami! Why am I registered in here?!"

"When did you even record us? I never even noticed..."

"It was embarrassing."

"Sis, why're you the only one who agreed to this...?"

Only one person's cheeks were getting beet red here.

"On top of that, it's installed with a system called the 'divine wind' feature, which will occasionally send a gust of air up from below. As such, I recommend wearing a skirt whenever you are running on the machine."

More like a divine panty flash feature.

"Are you crazy?!"

Ludie immediately sent a retort Nanami's way.

Honestly, that was dangerous. I was seconds away from showering Nanami with praise for such a brilliant addition.

"Of course, you are also able to adjust the force of the wind. There are three levels, the weakest being 'Territorial Infringement,' then 'Dignified Collapse,' and finally, 'Pure Nirvana.'"

"Oh, I see, 'Territorial Infringement'—what kind of arcane mumbo jumbo is that?!"

Now that I think about what that means for a sec...... Even the weakest "territorial infringement" is going to put everyone on display anyway, dammit!!!!

"Why is *that* what you're hung up on?! Who in the world would want a feature like that, anyway?!"

"Miss Ludie, I understand where your apprehensions are coming from. Did you think I wouldn't account for that as well? Please, there's no need to worry."

Chapter 6: A Dangerous Machine

"Right, well...obviously you would, right?"

"Of course. I made sure you'd be able to switch between cold and warm air for the gusts."

"That's! Not! The! Problem! Gaaaah! Who in the world would be worried about if it was hot or cold air coming up?!"

"Why would you want to be showered in warm air mid-run when you'd already be burning up...?"

"Uh, Takioto? That's not the issue here."

"She's right! The whole stupid wind feature is unnecessary! We're all going to be using this thing, too, so get rid of it immediately!"

"I'm terribly sorry, but I am unable to deactivate this function."

Yukine gently chided Ludie as she made even more complaints.

"Just calm down and think a moment, Ludie. The wind blows outside anyway, and as long as we don't wear a skirt, it's not even a problem."

She made an excellent point. For starters, no one would wear a skirt to go running on a treadmill in the first place. So could someone tell me where exactly this remorse I felt deep in my chest was coming from?

As things stood, it seemed like a convenient machine, and it looked to have plenty of the basic features expected from a treadmill. Not only that, but it apparently could add on extra weight with magic, so it was possible it could produce superior results to normal running.

However, there was still one thing that bothered me.

What was with all the buttons on the display?

"Nanami? What're all these buttons for?"

"That part of the machine remains a mystery, so I would ask you not to push them. However, it should be fine to press the buttons right in front of you."

"Did you even try to solve that mystery, or...?"

"Well, it was a used dungeon asset."

While part of me was terrified, my curiosity got the better of me, and I tried pressing one. When I did, a voice came out from the treadmill.

<*That's it, just like that! Yeeeeeah!!*>

"Oh, I get it, so it has a voice to cheer you on."

It didn't seem like a feature I'd get much use out of, but despite this, I pushed the button beside it.

<*Not bad, not bad at all.*>

What exactly was I supposed to be fighting here? I pushed the button next to that one.

<Yes, yes, take it alllllll off!>

<Now everything's on display!>

I instinctively looked around me. I felt like I was looking at a still frame frozen in time.

"Yeah, so we shouldn't go pressing any weird buttons."

I felt that deeply in my heart.

Chapter 7: The Hijiri Siblings

I'd definitely expected to get an unusual amount of attention if I went on campus.

But I had something to take care of at the Ceremonial Committee, and he had also asked me to come meet him, so I couldn't get out of the trip.

There was already someone waiting for me when I arrived at our meetup spot in the library.

"I've been waiting for you, Kousuke."

"*Tee-hee*, hey heeeey ♪!"

Greeting me were the Hijiri stepsiblings—Iori, a solemn look on his face, and Yuika, wearing the same bright smile as ever.

"Here you go, Iori."

"Thank you very much, Miss Sakura."

It appeared that Iori had already started one of the Student Council-related events and was helping sort the library. The fact that he was able to use this space and that the librarian, Rue Sakura, was bringing him coffee, signaled as much. It looked like Iori was getting through his events just fine.

I couldn't afford to sit around doing nothing, either.

"Here you go, Takioto… I've heard the rumors. I'm sure the Ceremonial Committee will be tough work, but give it all you've got, okay? If there's anything I can do—"

She then clenched her fists into a boxing pose and grinned.

"—I'll be sure to help you out!"

"Thank you."

After this, Miss Sakura left the room. The Academy's instructors knew about what the Ceremonial Committees activities entailed, of course. As the librarian, Miss Sakura was no exception.

However, Iori wouldn't have known the truth yet. I had done some behind-the-scenes maneuvering that hinted at it, though, so along with my induction announcement, he had probably guessed a certain amount of it already. He must have called me here to ask what my real intentions were.

It seemed he also understood that this was to be kept secret from the rest of the students, regardless of what the truth entailed. That explained why he'd asked Miss Sakura to let him use this place to hold our conversation.

Prompting Miss Sakura to share it with him.

"You got enough sugar? I had Nanami share some with me."

I took a bottle filled with sugar of various shapes form my item box and placed it in front of Iori.

Normally, Nanami would provide us with the sugar before we could even ask, but after thinking it over, I'd sent her home for this meetup.

She should be preparing for what was coming next at the moment. She was doing that, right?

Iori took off the lid and put an unbelievable number of cubes, hearts, stars, moons, and all sorts of adorably shaped sugar into his cup.

His younger stepsister Yuika looked on and heaved a big sigh.

"That sugar's super cute."

After making sure Iori had gotten his fill, I handed the bottle to Yuika, who seemed exasperated with her brother.

"You put in a whole sugar packet already!" she said, yet still picked one out from the bottle and mixed it in with her spoon.

I agreed that a cup of coffee was already plenty sweet with a single packet of sugar. But Yuika? Your brother here was putting in several times as much sugar *on top* of that single packet.

"Cute, right? Got them from Nanami. Lemme share some with you. Though I don't know if that'll be enough for the Hijiri household..."

Both Yuika and I turned to Iori. He brought his cup of black sugar water up to his mouth as if everything was perfectly normal. I'd stopped counting after his fifth cube. I hoped that he wouldn't end up with some disease in the future, but if worse came to worst, he could probably use magic to deal with it somehow.

"............I might grab some on the sly later. If my brother found out, he'd probably make off with most of it."

Iori would help himself if Yuika left it somewhere he could see. Maybe

▶ Chapter 7: The Hijiri Siblings

he'd even eat them straight. Nah, his sweet tooth couldn't be that bad... right?

"Makes me wonder what daily life is like in the Hijiri household..."

In the game, both Iori and Yuika stick to the dorms. There's almost no depiction of their homelife.

Yuika lit up at my question.

"What, does that mean you're interested in me?"

She absolutely knew that I hadn't made that comment with her in mind. Sending an adorably bright and flashy smile my way, she got closer to me—not just closer, but brought her entire chair up against mine while vigorously poking me in the arm.

Did she really think her bald-faced attempts at seduction were going to have an effect on me? Actually, she was so cute I was struggling to keep my thoughts from showing on my face. Did she get that? Her advances didn't just have an effect on me—they practically knocked me down for the count!

That being said, if you asked me if I was curious about the Hijiri household, I would say I was *incredibly* curious.

"I am, but right now there's something I'm far more interested in, see," I said, trying to dodge her question.

Yuika let out an over-the-top "Omigosh ♪!" before adding, "Well, I suppose if you insist, *tee-hee*. What do you want to ask me about first, my—"

"Yuika."

But she didn't go any further. Unable to watch his sister's act any longer, Iori scolded Yuika, prompting her to reluctantly give up on making a pass at me and sit down next to me.

So, uh, Yuika? Is it just me, or are you even closer now?

Watching her sit down, Iori sighed before finally bringing up the main subject of their meeting.

"Why did you join the Ceremonial Committee, Kousuke?"

"I mean, you must've seen it coming. And you were spot-on. That and, c'mon, you really don't still believe the Ceremonial Committee is some evil organization or something, do you?"

He couldn't possibly think otherwise. Iori looked firmly convinced of it. My remark should have been enough to tip him off.

"No, I know they're not..."

"Sorry for making you worry. Though, I normally can't go talking about this stuff, so no details. Just put up with vague answers for now, okay?"

The truth was, there were a few people outside the Three Committees who knew the truth anyway. Like the people working for the *Tsukuyomi Academy Newspaper*.

"So that really was how things were after all..."

Iori followed up with both an angry and relieved "Sheesh!" before looking me in the eyes and laughing.

"Guess it's totally obvious for some people, huh..."

"Of course it is. I mean, you were the one who came to Orange and me asking us to either ignore you or pretend we're on bad terms in the first place, Kousuke."

"The memory of you two rejecting the idea outright is still fresh in my mind."

I'd need to give a minimum amount of behind-the-scenes explanations to my classmates. I could've predicted that Orange would chat me up about the news anyway, asking something like, "The Ceremonial Committee? You're still you, right?"

Orange was a close friend, just like Iori.

"Besides, you'll hear all the details soon, whether I tell you or not."

"Huh? Why?"

"'Cause of the Student Council, yeah?"

Iori nodded with a serious look.

"I don't know if I'll be able to get it, but I'm doing my best."

"Oh, you'll get it. There's no way they won't want you. I guarantee it."

"You really think so?"

"Yup. Once you join, you can ask President Monica and Vice President Fran for the rundown on the Three Committees."

Iori acknowledged me with a nod before sighing. All of a sudden, he limply slinked back in his chair.

"......What's wrong? Did something happen between you and the heads of the Student Council?"

"No, that's not it. Both the President and the Vice President are very nice people. That's not the issue," he said, slightly adjusting his posture.

"I'm just sort of relieved."

"Relieved?"

"Since I knew that you weren't really that type of guy."

Iori relaxed his stiff cheeks into a smile.

"I'm so relieved I got to hear it from you directly."

"............My bad. I made you worry about me again, huh."

"Seriously, I'm so glad. I'll let it slide, though, since unlike last time, you at least went through the proper steps first."

"Whoa now, 'let it slide'? When did you start talking like a big shot all of sudden?"

Heck, at first, he'd done little more than passively observe everything from the sidelines, right?

"*Heh-heh-heh*," laughed Iori sheepishly.

"Well, I mean, I've been growing at lot, too, and all," he said, puffing out his chest.

After I drained my cup of coffee and watched Iori showboat, Miss Sakura came back to check on us.

"Would you like a refill?"

"Oh, Miss Sakura. Please."

Smiling, she poured more coffee into my cup.

"Hey, Miss Sakura. You've been working here a long time, right?"

"Yes, that's right. Is there something you'd like to ask me? Only my age is off limits," Miss Sakura said with a wink. While I was curious, I figured it'd be best to let sleeping dogs lie.

"I'd love to know, I'll admit, but that's not what I want to ask about. Do you have any dungeons you'd recommend students of our strength check out?"

"Dungeons......I sure do."

Miss Sakura recommended several different areas, and almost all of them were extremely important. Thinking ahead to the future, there was another place I wanted to get a handle on as soon as possible, too.

"I'll talk to Marino and have her change the coordinates on the teleportation circle for you, okay? You should be able to head there either tomorrow or the day after."

Iori and I thanked the winking librarian. Iori mentioned wanting to head into the fray as soon as we could.

From there, we pleasantly chatted for a little while, but then he was summoned by the Student Council. "Sorry, I was the one who called you here and everything," he said before departing in a fluster. That left...

"Guess it's time to head home."

"I suppose."

Just me and Yuika. We both cleaned up the coffee cups and thanked Miss Sakura before leaving the library together. Then, right as I was about to casually say "see ya," it crossed my mind...

Now that I thought about it, was Yuika's first event already over?

Judging from how she was carrying herself, I figured that it wasn't.

"Oh, right. Yuika."

"Hm? What's wrong? What are you giving me that super serious look for?"

"Just wanted to say, if you're ever in a tough spot or something, you should bring up my name. In the worst-case scenario, you can even use Marino...the principal's name, too. I'll be able to clear things up with her later."

It happened the second I spoke. I didn't miss the brief moment when her smile drooped slightly. That meant the event was unfinished.

"............Seriously, what's going on?"

"Anyway, just keep that in the back of your mind for me."

Iori would probably resolve the event at some point, but I figured I'd take some precautions. It was an early game event, so he'd have an easy time with it, and it'd probably all get squared away quickly.

As far as difficulty was concerned, the Saint and Sexy Scientist events were a whole lot more trouble. The latter brought a completely different kind of trouble with her, too.

For now, I figured I should run things by Marino.

"All right, then, I'm heading home," I said, turning my back to Yuika and continuing toward the teleportation circles. Then, right as I went to teleport to the school gate, I felt a tug on my stole from behind.

"Wait a second."

I could sense the slightest bit of hesitation in Yuika's clouded smile.

"Do you...know? Or maybe someone told you?"

Her expression suggested something wasn't sitting right with her.

Obviously, I knew all about what she was referring to.

"Nah. I just said that because you seemed to have something eating at you."

"That's not it," she mumbled with a sigh. "I'm not proud of it or anything, but the thing about me is, I'm pretty good at hiding stuff. At glossing over things, too, since usually people will believe me if I come up with some clever way to dodge their suspicions."

Yuika was exactly right. In-game, Iori learns about what's worrying Yuika only after an incident pops up.

"That's why I've never had anyone stand before me and talk like that before."

Her instincts were as sharp as ever. Despite that, I couldn't exactly explain myself in detail to her, either. After all, I knew things about Yuika that she currently didn't even know about herself.

"Wanna come to the Hanamura house?"

"Whooooa, this place is amazing."

"Take a seat wherever you'd like."

She sat down and looked around the area.

Claris brought us tea, and after I thanked her, she left to go shopping. Must have left out of consideration for Yuika.

"Looks like Nanami isn't the only beautiful maid you have serving you, huh."

"She's Ludie's maid."

"What?!"

Oh right, that would be news to her. Why would a maid of Her Highness Princess Ludivine be here?

"Ludie is living at the Hanamura house right now. We've got some straight-up monstrously powerful people here, see. Rock-solid security."

"I-I get it..."

Yuika's lukewarm smile made it unclear if that explanation really convinced her or not.

"Anyway, you wanted to talk to me about something, right?"

Yuika nodded with a strained smile.

"Do you know about my situation, Takioto?"

"Nope. I just figured you must've had a reason for transferring here."

"Really? You didn't hear anything from the principal?"

"Of course not. She's not the type of person to gossip about other people's private affairs willy-nilly."

The dirty jokes, though, those were incessant.

"......Why then?"

"I mean, it's pretty weird when you stop to think about it. Showing up at this specific school, this far into the year."

Yuika remained silent, but I continued.

"You're a really capable and strong person, that's for sure. Smart, too. You wouldn't have gotten into Susano Martial Arts Academy otherwise. And you definitely wouldn't have been able to transfer to Tsukuyomi Magic Academy, that's for sure."

Both institutions served the elite and the powerful.

"When I thought about why you transferred, it seemed fair to conclude that some sort of problem might've popped up at your old school."

"I came to Tsukuyomi because my brother goes there. Obviously, I've got a real brother complex going on... *Teh-heh*!"

"I'll agree with the brother complex part, but if that was the case, wouldn't you have applied to Tsukuyomi Magic Academy right from the start?"

A sad smile came to Yuika's face.

"So what happened, then? Something that couldn't be resolved at Susano Martial Arts Academy, I take it. I don't know for sure, but depending on the situation, I bet you thought the Hanamura family might be a really mighty connection to have on your side. Was that why?"

Of course, I could only make this inference because I knew Yuika's backstory.

For a few seconds, Yuika remained silent, with the same smile pasted on her face, until—

"........You're right. The truth is, I became the victim of this weird stalker."

—she began to broach the subject.

"A weird stalker?"

She nodded.

"A *very* weird stalker. The inside of my room got ransacked. But nothing was missing."

"Wait, ransacked, like a thief? But nothing was taken?"

"That's right, I still had all my magic items and money—even all my underwear was still there. Absolutely nothing was gone. That only made me even more afraid."

"Guess it wasn't a thief, huh. Was there anything else?"

▶ Chapter 7: The Hijiri Siblings

"There was this letter that just said 'I know who you are'…"

"That's terrifying. If you're being watched, then it's gotta be some pervert, right?"

I said this for now, but I knew the truth about who was behind it all. It was the work of a demon who was trying to use Yuika. They'd cloaked themselves in human form to exploit her for their own nefarious purposes, but she was able to escape by transferring schools. In the game, Iori then learns about all of this and gets rid of the demon for good.

"It's *suuuuper* creepy, right?!"

"Did you tell Marino about this?"

"Yup. She had just approached me about transferring, so I included this incident as part of why I wanted to come to Tsukuyomi. She approved the transfer pretty much immediately. She mentioned giving me a bodyguard, but I declined the offer since that seemed like going a bit too far."

"Very like Marino."

"She seriously got to work immediately, and I was able to get here in less than a week."

Suddenly, I felt a gnawing unease, like a small fishbone getting stuck in my throat. But I didn't understand where the discomfort was coming from.

"That's definitely fast. Nothing happened in the meantime?"

"I was shocked at how quick things went, too. But nothing of note happened afterwards. Partially because I avoided going out anywhere as much as possible, though."

She then changed the subject.

"In fact, Principal Marino actually mentioned you by name when we spoke."

"She did?"

"Yeah. She said, 'You can turn to Kou if you're ever in trouble' and 'That kid'll protect you for sure.'"

I got it now. That explained why I felt like Yuika was being extra chummy with me.

"Part of me also thought, hey, if I had one of the Hanamuras nearby, then maybe those weird stalkers wouldn't approach me."

It was all coming together. It made sense why she hung around me, too. Honestly, Yuika was just as cunning and sly as that Sexy Scientist was.

That reminded me, though...

"Wait, so then the fact you were with us when our classmates came to ask me about the Hanamura family..."

"I sorta started a bit of a rumor."

"That's a premediated crime if I ever heard one! Not that it's a really big deal or anything. But more importantly..."

"What?"

I needed to make sure I asked her the most important question of all.

"What became of that weird stalker?"

"I haven't heard anything from them since. I'm still a bit anxious about it."

"What? C'mon. You're fine."

"Why's that?"

"I mean, you've got Iori here with you, along with upperclassmen you can turn to, and even Marino. But most of all..."

"Most of all?"

"You've got me right here, too!"

"*Pfft*, seriously? You're a little bit more badass than I thought. You can't go saying stuff that'll make my heart skip a beat like that! I'll take my compensation fee now, thank you!"

"Why're you charging me for that?!" I said, and we both laughed.

"For real, though, let me know as soon as anything comes up, okay? I'll come flying to the rescue."

At this, Yuika played with her hair a bit, looking slightly embarrassed.

"Th-thank you."

Then she nervously looked around the room.

"Takioto, this thing over here's got me curious. Can I try it out?"

She must've wanted to change the topic. She pointed out the treadmill.

"Oh yeah, sure...... Actually, I haven't used it much myself yet."

"Really? Huh," she said before pressing the on button. Then she selected the "Guest" user option and started up the treadmill.

When she did, a holographic three-dimensional map projected before her.

"I guess I get to choose what course I want to take."

▶ Chapter 7: The Hijiri Siblings

Looking at Yuika as she got ready to start her run, I realized something.

"Wait. Hey, Yuika. Don't go running in your uniform."

At this, Yuika smiled mischievously and grabbed her skirt with her fingers.

"My, my, what's that, Takioto? You don't perhaps……want a peek, do you?"

If I had to choose between the two options, I would definitely want a peek, and would love to sear the memory into my brain twice over to ensure I'd never forget it.

"Stop, don't grab the hem of your skirt and make it flutter like that."

I could give her the fluttering skirt thing, sure, I get it. But why had she undone the ribbon on her uniform?! No, wait, calm down a second and think. The skirt fluttering didn't make any damn sense, either!

"It'll be fine, I'm not going to run that fast anyway… Let's see, I guess I'll go with a random course for now."

She pressed the buttons that appeared on the display one after another. It was then that I asked her a question that suddenly came to mind.

"Do you normally go running, Yuika?"

"Sure do! Not like, everyday though. Do you, Takioto?"

"Every single day. Sometimes, Yukine—the lieutenant of the Morals Committee—and I will go jogging together."

"Oh, is that so?" she replied, sounding rather uninterested, before beginning to run.

"It's basically just a normal treadmill, then, isn't it?" she said, touching the projected display with her finger and fiddling with the speed.

"…Hmm, what exactly is this button here? Let's see, 'Territorial Infringement,' 'Dignified Collapse,' and 'Pure Nirvana?' Between these three options, I've gotta go with 'Pure Nirvana,' right? Aaand, there!"

"It'll also do combat simulations, too, so if you'd like we could…… Wait, did you say 'Pure Nirvana'?"

The Pure Nirvana Yuika was talking about was *that* Pure Nirvana, right?

The wind generation system's strongest setting, the fantastic feature that guided all nearby gentlemen toward a Pure Nirvana of their own.

Yuika might not have been well-endowed enough for this to happen, but with someone of Ludie's size or bigger, the setting could showcase jiggling breasts together with the upskirt panty flash. It was like taking a drink of water after wandering through a blazing desert. Honestly, I had to tip my hat to Nanami for…… Uh, hold on a minute. Did Yuika just…press the "Pure Nirvana" button?

"No, Yuika, it's too dangerous!!"

"What're you talking about? It says 'Pure Nirvana,' right? P-u-r-e Nirvana!" she said with a smile. Just then, a magic circle appeared beneath the treadmill.

Surprised, Yuika tried to step off the machine and out of the magic circle, but she was blocked by some sort of invisible wall, as was the hand I extended in an attempt to save her.

"Excuse me?! What the hell is with this thing?!"

Yuika couldn't hide her panic, and I was honestly just as unsettled.

"No clue, but I'd sure like to know!"

"It's *your* machine! Why don't you know what it does?!"

She was right on the money. I wanted to ask Nanami the exact same thing myself.

All of a sudden, some text popped up on the display. Yuika read it aloud.

"Umm, let's see, soooo it looks like I'll be able to escape once I finish my running goal for the day… Oh, the machine started moving. Welp, I guess I have to start," she said, breaking into a run.

The only thought in my mind was how I would resolve this situation.

I had to let Yuika know the truth. But what exactly was I supposed to tell her? As I stood there internally conflicted, she started shouting.

"Whaaaat?! Wh-whoa, hold on! My skirt!"

It was the wind. That mischievous, naughty gust. The divine wind.

It showed up way too fast. It was already here.

"Seriously, what's with this thing?!"

Yuika desperately tried keeping her skirt down, but I saw them.

They were white.

Unquestionably white. It would have been wonderful to see Yuika push herself into wearing a more mature black. A warm, gentle pink would've probably suited her just as well, too. And while I was

Chapter 7: The Hijiri Siblings

sure the much-beloved blue-striped panties would look great on her as well, of course, white also looked fantastic. On top of that, today's briefs featured a vivid flower design on their lace section, a perfect fit.

"Takioto? Did you see them? You definitely saw, didn't you? Please just tell me you witnessed!!"

"Nope, I didn't see anything. Nothing at all... Just calm down, you're jumping to conclusions!"

"Come on! You obviously peeked. So what color were they?! Just guess if you have to, I don't care!"

"Why do you even want me to do that?!"

"Say something quick, I'm busy running here!"

"They were p-pink."

"Seriously? Obviously, they'd be black. Did you seriously not see them?! Why didn't you look, idiot?!"

"What, you're lying! They're white, aren't they?! Why the hell am I the one getting yelled at here?!"

"I *knew it*! You did look after all!"

"Gaaaaaaaaah! Leading questions aren't fair!"

"If you just honestly said you saw them, you could've made it out of this with just a nice, simple reincarnation."

"That still involves me dying once first, doesn't it?!"

"Ugh, seriously, what is with this frigid air blowing up at me! Is it trying to give me a cold or something?!"

"Yuika, there's no need to worry. You can at least change that into warm air instead!"

"What is changing the air temperature supposed to do? Please tell me *how* exactly that's supposed to put my mind at ease here! Hurry up and stop this thing, or I'm going to punch you into next week!"

She did have a point. I needed to compose myself.

There had to be a way I could control the machine... Remember what Nanami told us, Kousuke!

Uhhh.

"Oh right, if it's able to send data to the Tsukuyomi Traveler, then maybe you can control it from there, too?!"

"I don't care what you do, just hurry up and do it! Are you a tortoise or something?"

"Oh shush! Don't you know that the tortoise beat the hare?!"

That little dude just diligently kept on walking to beat the napping rabbit!

Access via Tsukuyomi Traveler. Yes, yes, this was it!

"Great, I'm connected! Let's see, five foot four inches tall, around ninety po—"

"Excuuuuuuse me?! Why the heck are you reading out my height and weight?!"

"S-sorry, my bad."

Okay, okay, controls, controls...

"So this thing popped up that looks like a control panel, and, well..."

"Really?! Oh my gosh, Takioto, you must be a genius!"

"Aww shucks, you're too kind," I joked while fiddling with the controls.

"Haven't you ever heard of sarcasm before?! Hurry up and shut this off!"

"Of course I have, geez! Look, I want to turn this thing off just as quickly as you do, but there are so many buttons...and there's no explanation about what they do!"

At just a cursory glance, there were over ten buttons to choose from. And what was this knob-looking thing? On top of that, there was a scroll wheel even farther down, too.

"I can't hold out much longer, so hurry up and press a random button! Do something!"

"Got it, got it! Here I go!" I said before pressing down the button that looked the easiest to press.

<Yes, yes, take it alllllll off!>

Sudden silence. An exchange of glances. Twitching lips.

"Wh-wh-what are you fooling around with?! Are you asking to get punched silly?!"

"No, you got it all wrong. I was trying to turn it off."

<Everyone's got their own secret thoughts on the inside, see?>

"Huuuuh?!"

"It's not me, I swear it's not me. The machine's saying all that stuff on its own!"

<Heh-heh, now that's *a view*.>

"*Gaaaaah*! I'm not doing a bit here, you know?! I'm not looking for you to 'yes-and' me, either! Don't you get my life's on the line?! What the hell are you doing?!"

"Just stay calm, okay? How about this button that's a little bit removed from all the others?"

<Magic circle color has been changed to pink.>

"What's changing that supposed to accomplish?!"

"Ooookay, okay, calm down, it's important to stay level-headed. For now, I'll just try pressing all the buttons at once...... I wonder what this knob's for?"

<Temperature has increased by one degree.>

"What did I just say?! Who cares about the damn wind temperature!"

"O-okay, then, uh, what about this?!"

<Speed increased.>

"Hey, uh, Takioto? You're not just pretending to help me and actually *trying* to trap me in here, right? Please tell me you're not!"

"Of course not!"

Ah, screw it, time to let loose! I'd hit all of them! Whatever happened, I didn't care anymore!

<The emergency super-perverted sexy lewd naughty time button has been pressed.>

"Excuuuuuuuuuuuuuuuuse me?! Hoooooooooold on now, what the hell did you press?!"

"Whoa, whoa, it's not my fault, it's not my fault! Outta my control! An accident!"

"Uhhhhh?! The wind in here's got a real murderous vibe all of a sudden?!"

She was right. The gusts of wind coming out of the machine were vaguely blade-shaped...

Except in reality, this wasn't a murderous wind—it was a hot and sexy wind. An erotic wind. The gale ripped Yuika's clothes to shreds, like a mischievous dust devil.

Nah, it was a divine wind to me.

"You better remember what you've done, okay? You'll remember, right? Don't you dare forget!"

I would remember that pure white for the rest of my life.

<Entering Sensitivity Amplification mode.>

"What now? What's 'sensitivity amplification' supposed to be? What the heck is it?! Oh, an explanation popped up on the screen. Let's see then, it says here, 'Please be aware that if you do not clear your distance goal within a set time, a gas will be released that will amplify your sensitivity between two to a maximum of three thousand times its normal state.' Uh, so what's 'sensitivity amplification,' then?!"

"I mean, when you're talking about 'sensitivity amplification'...... there's only one explanation."

Obviously, there was really only one thing the term brought to mind for eroge players. A genius idea. Except it was the stuff of *fantasy*, right?

How ridiculous. Something like that would never exist in real life. If it did, though, you can bet your ass it'd get my fire going, that's for sure! *Wah-hah-hah-hah...!*

"Wait, noooooooooooo!"

Uh oh. Crap, crap, crap! Now we were in *real* trouble, gaaaaaaah...!

"Wh-what was that about?!"

"Hurry, Yuika. You need to hurry. Run like your life depends on it!"

This was an eroge world, a place that had made me offer up used panties on an altar! That gas really could end up making her body three thousand times more sensitive!

"Huh, but why?! Takioto, what's going on?!"

Now wasn't the time for whys or buts. In an eroge, the word *sensitivity* meant one thing—sexual sensitivity. And this thing was going to increase Yuika's three thousand times over! Even the brawniest ninja in the world couldn't withstand something like that!

"Just shut up and sprint! If that gas starts blowing, you'll get hornier than a dog in heat!"

"H-horny?! Why're you bringing up weird stuff like that all of sudden?! Are you high or something? Well, I guess you're just strange all the time, but... How am I supposed to make any sense out of this weird butterfly-effect nonsense?!"

The gas was going to amplify your body's sexual sensitivity, okay? Three *thousand* times over, too. Not two or three, but three times one thousand, three thousand times! She'd cum just from feeling the clothes on her skin!

She'd be descending from Pure Nirvana into a Living Hell! Hell was coming—literally!

"*Hnraaaaaauugh!*"

▶ Chapter 7: The Hijiri Siblings

I immediately filled my stole with mana and sent a punch straight into the invisible wall around her.

"Yuikaaaaaaaaa, Yuikaaaaaaaaaa. Yuuuuikaa… Dammit! C'mon, what the hell's this thing made of, anyway?!"

"T-Takioto? Um, you've got snot and tears running down your face. But why're you smiling like a creep, too?! Anyway, calm down. I just need to keep running to the end!"

I listened to Yuika's words, turning over their meaning in my head. She had a point.

"Y-yeah, yeah, you're right!"

Of course! She just needed to finish running!

"Go, Yuika! Go, go, Yuika, you totally got this! You can do it! You're the best in Japan! I'll give you everything I've got, my burniiiing heaaaaart!"

"What did I juuuuuust say?! Calm down, Kousuke, I'm doing the best I can here!"

"Still, who knows what could happen next!"

Life was like that. You might suddenly get in an accident, or your father could keel over out of the blue. The company you clocked out of yesterday might go under overnight.

But in eroge, everything happened for a reason. That was why this whole nightmare dance had started, right? Which was why I was so uneasy. This anxiety was definitely justified, okay?!

"It's going to be fine, seriously. See, look, my body's starting to feel lighter, and I'm gradually whittling down on the distance, too. Hm? It smells sort of sweet all of sudden… Hey, what's up with this pink smoke?"

"What did I literally just warn you about?!"

"So how's that explain the pink gas? Wait, this isn't…? Ah…… This has to be a joke, right?"

Yuika's heart rate must have shot up. She was pressing down on her chest with one hand, and her breathing had gotten much heavier.

"U-unhh, uuuuuhn……Haaaaaahn!"

"Run, Yuika, run! Hurryyyyyy!"

At this, Yuika picked up speed in a panic.

"Haah! Haaannnhhhh! Nghhhh! Ahh! Aaaaaaaahn!"

—and that's when it happened. The rare yet all-too-common wind buffeted her from below.

"Eeeeeeeeek!"

A full display of white—*très magnifique*!

"Whhhy did this strong gust have to shoot up right noooow?!"

Oh boy, was it strong. And oh boy, was it tearing everything apart—she wasn't going to be able to keep anything covered up now. In fact, I had gotten a view of everything in the whirlwind that had sliced up her clothes a few moments ago.

Yuika looked like Venus incarnate. She had a plump, well-shaped butt. Cute lacy underwear. A beautifully pale and slender body, tinged slightly red. Her clothes were totally see-through. Sweat was splattering off her.

"How pretty……"

"*Haah, haaaaah*, just what the hell are you getting lost in thought about?!"

Pure Nirvana indeed. Except my mind was shot to hell, and any purity of the nirvana was gone. Sorry, Yuika, but I didn't think I'd be much help now.

"Yuika………… Good luck."

She finished her run about ten minutes later.

Her target distance reached, Yuika emerged from the clutches of the machine, covered in wounds.

She sat down with her legs bent and splayed to the sides, face dyed red and gasping for breath. Her uniform was a disaster, having been torn to shreds by the wind blades. Her chest was exposed, and her white panties could be seen from the gaps in her torn skirt. She seemed to still be under the effects of the sensitivity amplifications, too; every so often, a shiver would take hold of her entire body.

Sweat was running down her face even now, flowing all the way down to the nape of her neck. Her eyes were filled with tears.

I could also see sweat beading on her thighs, dripping down from the skirt that was no longer able to fulfill its proper duty. It sort of looked like she had clashed with a powerful opponent. But the truth was that she'd simply gone for a run. Though I suppose she had fought a fearsome foe of sorts, albeit an unconventional one.

Yuika averted her gaze when she noticed me looking at her. She didn't have an ounce of strength left.

I silently held out a towel. Mumbling and grumbling to herself, she accepted it.

Chapter 8 — Dungeon: Archives of Promise

I thought it was strange that Yuika hadn't come to our meetup spot, nor gotten in touch.

Iori hadn't replied after I messaged him to ask if he knew if something was up, either. Maybe he'd delved into that dungeon Miss Sakura recommended to us. Whether it was more "time is money" or more "striking while the iron is hot," Iori was very quick to act. Not that this was a bad thing.

On top of that, it seemed that Iori had enlisted Ludie, Katorina, Class Rep, and Orange to go in along with him. Ludie had mentioned it that morning, so I wasn't likely to get a reply from any of them, either.

I sort of felt like my classmates were excluding me, but I already had plans today with the Ceremonial Committee, so I wouldn't have been able to join them regardless.

None of that was really the issue here, though.

"Yuika sure is taking her time..."

Even if she was running late, she should've shown up by now. The time we'd agreed to meet up had long since passed. After that giant mess yesterday, I couldn't help admiring her for calling to meet me like this, but I assumed she was probably going to make me treat her to something as an apology.

Personally, I thought that was being too tolerant if that was all it took to settle things. If I were Yuika, I'd punch Kousuke in the face.

These thoughts swirling in my head, I looked down at my Tsukuyomi Traveler to see a message suddenly pop up.

It was from Shion. We'd just had a meeting in the library, so it must have concerned what we'd discussed. The Moon Court could've worked as our meetup spot just fine, but I had something I wanted to take care of, so I had her change it. As I replied, I happened to think back to Nanami.

"Nanami's really doing a good job."

I had asked the maid to take care of quite a few things for me. Not just dungeon surveyance, but information gathering, too. She was also making sure to ask Ms. Ruija for help, too, right?

"She really is taking her time..."

Despite it all, Yuika still wasn't here. Nor could I get in touch with her. For the time being, I thought I'd try looking around the places she might be and message her that I was heading elsewhere.

When I reached the teleportation circles, I found several people making a scene.

"What's wrong?"

I asked this of a fox-eared beastfolk nearby, and she jumped in surprise. Then she took one look at my face and got even more surprised.

"Um, well, I thought I heard a girl screaming. I went looking for her and saw a brown-haired first-year being dragged onto the teleportation circle... It all happened in a flash."

Hearing this, I couldn't help letting out a loud, "Huh?!" That was definitely a kidnapping, right?

"*Eep!*"

"Ah, whoops, sorry. I wasn't trying to scare you."

I seriously wasn't trying to frighten her. But she'd said the girl had brown hair, didn't she ...?

"Hey, did that girl have a side ponytail?"

The girl looked stunned, and my head reeled for a moment. I immediately took out my Tsukuyomi Traveler, said Yuika's name, and pressed the call button.

"Do you know which circle she stepped in?"

"O-oh, uh, that one there, I think...," she said, pointing toward a teleportation circle with a simple piece of paper stuck to it reading, *Currently mid-connection and unavailable for use.*

I had definitely seen this before.

Ending the call as it switched to voicemail, I got the attention of the second-year student standing in front of the teleportation circle who appeared to be guarding it.

"*E-eek!* Kousuke Takioto?!"

Letting out a brief, weird yelp, she shouted my full name before covering her mouth.

"Have you contacted Marino...er, the principal and the teachers yet?"

"Oh, yes. We tried a few moments ago, but we couldn't get in touch with the principal..."

"Did you see her get carried off?"

"Erm, no, I'm sorry."

It probably seemed like I was bullying this poor girl. Nevertheless, now wasn't the time to be worrying about how people perceived me.

"I was just asking. Let me through."

"But we still haven't made sure this route's safe yet..."

"Let me through."

Sidestepping the second-year girl, I jumped over the simple fence using my Third Hand as support. Then I headed straight into the teleportation circle.

While they also connected to dungeons on the campus grounds, the Tsukuyomi Academy magic circles could link up to dungeons in other locations as well. This one connected to a dungeon outside of the Academy, so they were likely stopping people from using it because it wasn't totally safe on the other side yet.

On the other end of the teleportation circle there was a well-worn brick building. I instantly applied my enhance magic and walked through the entrance.

Inside was a large stone monument, on which was a picture of a single woman bowing her head to an angel.

In the middle of the room was yet another teleportation circle, but I walked past it to try touching the wall instead.

Yet my hand just passed through it.

It was an illusory magic wall. I continued forward with a gulp, knowing that this was the worst thing that could have happened.

"Dammit. They had to go activating this teleportation circle, too..."

I had to admit—things were as bad as they could get.

This was one of the dungeons Miss Sakura had recommended to me. A dungeon I would need to clear at least two times to complete certain events.

But it seemed that Yuika had accidently fulfilled the requirements to unlock it.

"And now it's opened up. Actually, wait, maybe that was the goal here?"

I needed to remember how the Yuika Hijiri event played out.

Yuika Hijiri had transferred to this school to escape a "weird" stalker. That "weird" stalker's true identity was a demon. Why exactly she has a stalker at all is never made clear in the game because Iori ends up defeating them.

Though I couldn't say for sure, I had a hunch about why the demon had been stalking her. If I was right, and they had come to this dungeon with that in mind, then…

"This could be as rough as it was with Ludie."

The absolute worst possible outcome. That was where things were heading.

The only silver lining was that I was here. I had to be the one here. In which case, the first thing I needed to do was…

"*Huuuuu, hoooooo.*"

Take a deep breath and think things over. What was the best way to go about this?

I would be fine heading straight into the dungeon where I believed Yuika had been taken.

However, the fact that there was a magic circle here meant that another event had already been triggered as well.

Clearing this solo……was probably possible. The surefire option, though…

"I should call for someone to help and be prepared to fall a bit behind. But I don't want to be waiting here for long."

In which case, who was best to call? I reached out to Yukine while I thought things over.

Dammit. This couldn't have happened at a worse time. Now that I thought about it, had it been a mistake to ask Nanami to handle those favors for me? No, I couldn't let her confront them yet. She would instantly realize who we were up against, and there was no telling what might transpire if I forced her into this encounter.

Yukine didn't answer my call. Marino……didn't get through, either. I supposed it was time to try phoning Sis.

What if she didn't pick up? I wanted to reach out for help, but I needed someone who was free. Someone strong, who'd come immediately no

▶ Chapter 8: Dungeon: Archives of Promise

matter how off the wall the situation sounded. Asking some random students for help would be futile.

Suddenly, two faces popped into my brain.

They had said it themselves, hadn't they? To reach out if I was ever in trouble. I had already met up with them once today, and they had both laid out their schedules for me, too.

I dashed off and used the teleportation circle to return to the Academy before immediately hopping into another teleportation circle. However, this time I was headed......to the library, where we had just met.

I took off running toward my destination—one of the rooms inside the library—as soon as I arrived.

Fortunately, Shion and Minister Benito were both still there. Shion was in the middle of taking a bite of red bean jelly, but when I suddenly burst through the door, she was so startled that her food nearly fell to the floor before she managed to catch it with her plate.

"W-well, well now? And what's got you in a rush? You scared me out of my socks," Shion said as she placed her plate back on the table. Minister Benito looked at my panic and cocked his head.

"What's the matter?"

I would've liked to apologize to Shion for making her jump, or maybe purposefully tease her about it, but I didn't have the time for any of that right now.

I quickly moved in front of the pair and bowed.

"I need your help."

They both looked at me stunned, eyes wide in blank surprise.

—Shion's Perspective—

"Well now, we can't stand for that, can we?"

My breath caught in my throat seeing Minister Benito mutter that through a fake smile. He was clearly roiling on the inside.

Of course, I was just as incensed myself. It was a tense situation indeed.

After sending along a message to one of the instructors who could handle things quickly, we hurried toward the dungeon, watching Kousuke's long stole flutter in front of us all the while.

Why, I would say that ludicrously long scarf of his would instantly come to mind for most people when they heard his name. It was always just barely flowing over the ground, yet mysteriously, I had never seen a speck of dirt on it.

This held true even within the walls of a dungeon.

I nearly fell to my knees when I heard that Kousuke was almost always sending mana into his stole, imbuing it with a downright abnormal level of strength. If the average fellow tried such a feat, they'd be a dried-out mummy within the hour.

Witnessing him in combat only made me even more flabbergasted.

I'd heard he used his stole as a weapon, of course, and that he utilized it like an extra limb.

But never in my wildest dreams would I have imagined that he had the strength to charge forward while repelling every single one of his foes' attacks or beat them into submission with a crushing punch from above.

Why, if I had to liken his form to something, it would have to be an armored vehicle. Not any armored vehicle, mind you, but one with blades attached to the sides.

"Let's head to the next floor," he said, returning his katana to its sheathe. He pushed onward without giving the magic stones the enemy had dropped so much as a glance. How terrifically sharp his blade was.

"He has an intriguing style of fighting, wouldn't you say? Yet it's quite rational, too." Minister Benito murmured this as we followed after Takioto.

"Quite so."

"He's almost too promising, really."

I could only nod along with the Minister's words.

It was plain as day, too, that his extra emphasis, that he was in fact *too* promising, was not only in regard to his physical strength.

"They'll show up on this floor," Takioto said, taking some item from his pocket and filling it with mana.

He then set his sights on the freshly approaching creatures, two snake-shaped demons with angel wings growing out from their sides.

The sigiled stone in his hand glowed crimson, and he summoned a magic circle to send a small fireball flying toward the monsters.

▶ Chapter 8: Dungeon: Archives of Promise

"Leave the left to me. Shion, the enemy on the right's weak to dark magic."

Hearing this, I promptly started my incantation. Minister Benito stepped out in front of me and reflected the light arrows the snake fired toward me.

"Shadow."

When I cast my spell, a circular shadow formed at my feet, around three feet in diameter.

"Go forth."

Right as the words left my lips, the shadow flew behind the snake. Then, watching for the moment the snake launched his next attack, I transformed the magic's shape.

"Emerge, and seize it."

As I spoke, a large black hand appeared from within the shadow and took hold of the snake, hovering in the air. This serpent creature let forth a strange cry, but I paid it no heed.

"Crush it."

With this, the black hand slammed the snake down against the floor. It appeared the impact was enough to kill the monster.

Takioto had already taken care of his side of things as well.

"It looks like demons are weak to fire, huh? Did you know that?"

Minister Benito posed the question to me. I shook my head, of course. Though the Minister didn't voice it aloud, the two of us likely had the same thoughts on our mind.

I couldn't help my shock. I had never once met a monster like this, yet Takioto instantly saw through its true nature before attacking its weakness with precision.

Dungeons and monsters were multifarious. When visiting a labyrinth for the first time, one would often encounter monsters they had never seen before, and the only option was to either gather information before jumping into battle, or to spend time researching them yourself.

That was well and good, but did Kousuke have the time to gather any of that information? Or the time to spend researching these monsters?

Certainly not.

Assuming he was already informed about them from the start, that would mean he had an enormous amount of knowledge to his name.

Chapter 8: Dungeon: Archives of Promise

Just how much did he know?

"Let's go."

I hadn't even noticed that Takioto had defeated another monster. He again urged us onward.

Kousuke Takioto claimed he was panicked about Yuika's kidnapping, yet from my perspective, he appeared nothing but calm and levelheaded.

"This dungeon is nothing but books and more books, isn't it?"

It was if a someone had turned a library into a labyrinth. The bookshelves served as its walls, and it was impossible to take any of the tomes from them. On top of this, the stacks were exceedingly sturdy. I couldn't fathom what they were made of, but they weren't going to collapse any time soon.

"I know there are dungeons whose walls are full of weapons, but I didn't know there were places like this, too."

"I wish we could spend a bit more time getting a good look at them all," Takioto said, replying to Minister Benito's comment as he continued forward.

According to Takioto's assessment, this dungeon was consistent with other fixed encounter-style dungeons, where monsters appeared as you advanced to the next floor.

He'd also insisted that there were no wandering monsters in this labyrinth, either. Admittedly, our trio had yet to meet any.

The Minister and I followed after Takioto. Trailing behind him, we passed through a number of halls and corridors before he suddenly looked around the area.

"Huh......"

A mysterious room, indeed. Up until now, there had only been bookshelves on the walls, but here there was a table, along with a freestanding bookshelf. Stacked up on the table were even more tomes.

Takioto stopped in front of what looked like a teleportation circle in the back of the room. It was plain as day that we would need to activate this magic circle to advance.

"It looks like there's something written in the ancient language here."

"Can you read it, Minister?"

"I can pick out words. I see that 'book' and 'magic circle' are written here, but..."

"Shion, Minister Benito. Let's put these titles back up on the shelf,"

Takioto said, taking one of the books and sliding it into one of the empty spaces on the bookshelf.

"Can you read what it says, then?"

"I haven't read it in detail. But I'm guessing that putting the books in here will open the way for us," he said before he swiftly crammed the tomes into the open shelf spaces.

That was indeed a possibility. Thus, we too went to return the books to their shelves.

"Well, it does seem like they all fit on this bookshelf, doesn't it?"

Despite the other books being harder than hard, impossible to grab off the shelves, these ones slipped right in place without issue. Though most were indecipherable on account of being written in the ancient script, the color and thickness of their spines went a long way in providing a clear destination for them. Without this visual clue, I wouldn't have been able to lift a finger.

Immediately after we finished returning all the books, it happened.

The shelf rumbled and started sinking into the floor. I had my fan in my hand, and though I readied another shadow, it proved unnecessary.

"The way is open," Minister Benito murmured.

The teleportation circle leading to the next layer was now shining bright.

However, we didn't immediately talk about moving on. First, we made time for a break of sorts, albeit a short one, just barely long enough, or perhaps not, to enjoy a cup of tea.

Granted, I supposed we had barely engaged in any combat as it was. I wasn't very fatigued.

Nevertheless, our short rest furnished me the opportunity to consider many things.

Kousuke Takioto was a monster, and he'd done everything in his power to get that way.

I myself believed that those who were simply smart, with little else to show for themselves, often mulled over things without ever taking action. They didn't take a single step forward. And because they refused to act, they brought nothing about.

In such instances, a blockhead who didn't pause to think things through was sometimes the better option. Simpletons though they were,

▶ Chapter 8: Dungeon: Archives of Promise

they *could* take the first step forward. And while failure might have visited them often, they would sometimes get lucky enough for things to fall into place or be blessed with friends who helped them succeed.

This boy, Kousuke Takioto, had everything—knowledge, talent, and skills. Those were impossible to attain without effort, of course. Above all else, however, he cared about his friends and possessed more initiative than any ignorant simpleton.

In which case, he was sure to succeed.

To the ignorant outsider, he may have looked a fool himself, but that couldn't have been further from the truth. Clearly, he'd calculated things ahead of time so he could act with purpose. That was how he'd set records that even the Minister or I—that no one, rather—could ever hope to best.

Nanami had claimed her master would become the strongest of all, and he might indeed do just that. Between him and the President, I couldn't say who would emerge the more powerful.

That woman's strength was plain as day.

Overwhelming strength that surpassed all the other Academy students without exception, a charisma that could engender anyone's loyalty, enviously beautiful features, outstanding academics even among students in her year. The President was basically perfect.

Both Minister Benito and the Saint's strength were equally easy to pinpoint and understand. Fran and Yukine, too. Their strength was clearly visible.

Meanwhile, this boy had his own easily understood strength, yes, but he also seemed to possess inscrutable power and knowledge, reminiscent of Anemone.

"Perplexing indeed."

"Shion?"

"Forgive me, I just had something on my mind."

"I see. I've been thinking over something a bit myself… Looks like the next floor's come into view."

At that, we faced forward.

"The next floor, huh…"

I was puzzled to hear Takioto mutter that to himself with such significance.

However, I didn't have time to inquire any further.

"Well now, looks like we've got ourselves quite the spirited one, don't we?" Minister Benito commented.

We stopped and stared at the thing directly in front of us.

"Now this fellow I've seen before."

Standing there was a giant, close to nine feet tall. His muscular form had no excess fat to speak of, and his arms were quite wide, a testament to his strength. His body odor was suffocating.

"A titan, huh. A regular one, but he has quite the impressive weapon."

What a dauntless opponent. While I hadn't the slightest intention on losing to a thing like this, we were definitely in for a hard-fought battle.

"We can bring him down. I'll act as a shield and... Huh?"

Suddenly, Takioto started to panic mid-sentence. It was completely unlike anything I had seen from him before. He then started muttering under his breath about something.

"Calm yourself. What's going on?"

After I spoke, Takioto asked me to look over to the teleportation circle beyond the titan.

Glancing where he directed me, I saw a teleportation circle, a pedestal of some sort, and...

"Is that a bright red liquid I see?"

"And a fair amount of it, too."

I finally grasped what had driven Takioto to panic. He must have assumed that liquid was Yuika's blood.

It was at that exact moment that Minister Benito grabbed Takioto by the shoulder.

"Whoa now, careful. You have to look before you leap."

Takioto had seemed on the verge of sprinting off, but Minister Benito held him back. Then Takioto began to speak, a grave look on his face.

"I haven't gotten into gear yet."

In other words, he was saying he hadn't planned on charging in.

I could tell there was an intoxicating amount of mana filling up his stole. Naturally, it wasn't being directed at me, but just thinking about such a possibility sent a shiver down my spine.

Yet the Minister had told that intimidating presence to calm down.

"Takioto. I don't think that titan there's going to let us stroll past him."

It was as Minister Benito had said. Titans were quite fast on their feet. Even if we were able to pass beside him, as long as the teleportation circle sat behind his back, we'd need to distract him somehow.

"Shion."

The Minister called for me with a solemn look in his eye. He had dropped his usual lighthearted tone.

"Yes?"

"I'm leaving Takioto with you," he said before activating a body enhancement spell.

"After I beat this guy, I'll head over to wherever you end up. Both of you can go on ahead."

He slicked back his hair.

"Our goal here's to rescue Yuika, right?"

Takioto nodded.

"So then think about if she could actually clear this dungeon herself. Definitely not, right? Even if she managed to do something about the kidnapper that dragged her here, she wouldn't be able to then get through the whole place, right?"

Minister Benito continued.

"In that case, we'll have to clear this dungeon to save her. That got me thinking about what we'll need to do to continue our expedition. But then it hit me: There's something we're gonna need no matter what."

I shifted my gaze from Minister Benito over to Takioto.

"Knowledge. That means you, Takioto. You can solve the puzzles in this dungeon. And you're not just good for that. You're strong, too."

"Be that as it may, we don't have much time left," I said, staring at the titan. This must've been why Benito told me he was leaving Takioto in my hands.

"Will you manage on your own?"

"And just who do you think you're talking to?" he replied, trying to show off, before approaching the monster.

"I may not look the part, but I'm still the Minister of the Ceremonial Committee, you know."

One step, then one more.

The sword in his hand was enchanted with the earth element, enshrouded in an almost golden mana glow. He must have still been channeling mana into the blade, for the light continued to grow even brighter.

"Takioto. I wanted to play the knight in shining armor and save the captured princess, but it looks like I'll be passing that off, too."

"Minister Benito......"

"But," he continued, "I want you to save Yuika no matter what it takes. If it truly looks like there's nothing you can do, then I need you all to hold out by any means necessary. If you can do that…"

Benito turned half his face back toward us.

"I'll come save you. No matter what."

At this, he kicked back hard against the ground.

The titan stared at Benito as he ran toward him and let out a loud growl.

The titan swung his enormous mountain hatchet down at his sprinting target, but Benito made sure to meet it with his own sword.

From the clash came an explosive metallic clang. Then something came rushing past me. Power on power. The impact of their clash had turned into vibrations that were passing through my very skin.

"Go, both of you!"

Benito had blocked his head on the downward swing of the hatchet, sent from that colossal, nearly nine-foot-tall frame. We ran past him and continued toward the teleportation circle.

After we teleported, Takioto looked back at the circle for a brief moment, but once I called to him that we needed to hurry, we finally ran onward.

Minister Benito really was the guy I knew.

He was a stud. Both physically and emotionally. This was how he'd garnered popularity with eroge players despite being a male character.

I was running down the corridor when Shion called out to me.

"We're remaining calm, yes?"

"Yup. I'm extremely level-headed right now."

The titan Benito was squaring off against was this dungeon's miniboss. Depending on the situation, it could be an even stronger enemy than the actual boss, which lurked deeper in the dungeon.

"Come now, the Minister will be perfectly fine, so you don't need to fret over him. Why, he's one of the top five most skilled students in the Academy. If anything, we should hurry along, before he catches up to us in a flash."

To be honest, I'd brought both Benito and Shion along with me to find a way of dealing with the titan. I was surprised that Minister Benito had insisted on soloing it, but he'd make it out all right.

The more pressing problem at hand was Yuika.

"Shion, we're almost at the next floor, but I've got a bad feeling about this."

"Is that so?"

In this dungeon, the Archives of Promises, there's a path that continues on once you fulfill some conditions. You need to fight several of a specified enemy before you can head into a room farther on in the dungeon that triggers an event.

If that enemy was the same as it was in-game, then they should be on this next floor, but… They'd prove troublesome if I tried fighting them solo. I prayed that they wouldn't be the ones to show up, but the titan's appearance already lined up with the in-game version of the dungeon.

"And there they are."

I had figured it would play out this way.

"Well, well, well. This looks like another vexing obstacle indeed."

Waiting for us was a large group of monsters. However, there were only two different types among them. The first species was the snake that we had encountered along the way; there were at least several tens of them in total. Farther down, we could make out a demon-looking individual wielding a staff.

There, situated beside it, I could see the path that headed toward the next floor.

"There's so many of them, and once they take off…"

It was the worst. It made me recall the harpies from the Tsukuyomi Academy Dungeon.

"I do wish to get to Yuika as soon as possible, but punishing these serpent louts will take quite some time… Kousuke?"

"What is it? Wait—ow!"

When I turned around, my chin smacked into her fan.

"Are you staying calm, then?"

She must have been worried that I was just as panicked as I had been back in the titan's room.

"I'm okay," I said, prompting Shion to stare at me hard in the eyes.

You can get there yourself, no?

She didn't say it directly, but I could hear her voice in my head.

"Of course. I'm counting on you, Shion. Once this if over, I'll treat you to the most expensive red bean jelly around."

I cracked a joke to try setting her mind at ease. Shion replied with a big smile. "Such nonsense. Why would I need that?" *Though*, she continued, "Go ahead and show me and Yuika what a man you are instead!"

I couldn't help but smile. She'd told me to show her what a man I was, but—

"Whoa, whoa, come on, Shion. I'm already a pretty manly specimen as is, right?"

"Sure, I'll admit that you have about a pinky's worth of manliness in you now, but I'd say you need some extra oomph."

While she spouted such silliness, Shion began building up her mana.

"Now then, I suppose here's where I'll send this whole area flying with some magic. You better go and save Yuika, you hear me? If you can't manage that, why, I'll go announce your lack of a backbone to the entire school!"

An impossible feat for me, ill-equipped to take on many opponents at once.

"I'm not missing a backbone. It's just that it seems lacking when compared to yours, Shion. Or smaller, I should say."

"Your backbone's small? And pray tell, what is that supposed to mean? Surely you're not trying to suggest that I have a large rear, are you?"

"Oh, definitely. Just my type."

I didn't deny it. Staring, a bit taken aback by my response, Shion then finally burst into laughter.

"Hah-hah! Hah-hah-hah-hah-hah-hah-hah! Hah-hah-hah-hah! Comedy, pure comedy, indeed. Here I thought Nanami was the only one with a sharp tongue, but I see you give her a run for her money yourself."

After her bout of laughter, her expression grew serious.

"I liked that, yes indeed. Liked it quite a bit, I'd say. Say, Takioto...... Hmm, that's a wee bit stiff, and doesn't really suit you now, does it? Kousuke? No, not quite that, either. What about Kou, then...? Perfect. Kou?"

"Yes?"

"Ready?"

Of course.

I dashed into the fray. A number of eyes all shifted toward me.

Then, each began their incantations.

I walloped one close to where I stood, swinging at another nearby snake as I advanced forward. While I did, the annoying ophidians looked to have finished their incantations, and they rained their arrows of light down on me without even giving me a chance to breathe.

I deflected the unending volley of light arrows with my stole and evaded them every now and then. It was almost like a meteor shower pouring from above. Only this was far brighter than any real meteor shower.

"Good job buying time," Shion said quietly, activating her mana and launching the spell she had prepared.

"Kou, take a good look. This here is my dark magic."

A scarlet line arced up into the air. It wasn't just one line, either. In the span of a millisecond, more appeared with it, then yet more, until there were far too many to count.

Then the multitude of scarlet lines all formed into the shape of a massive flower.

"Red Spider Lily."

The red flower tore the monsters to shreds. The snakes hit by the scarlet magic produced a sizzling sound, like they were melting, and fell to the ground writhing in agony.

Their wounds were charred pitch black. That blackness then spread across their bodies, until it eventually consumed them entirely, dissolving them into magic particles.

"Now, go!"

I rushed through the path Shion had opened for me.

Red Spider Lily was a unique spell that only Shion was capable of using. If it hit you, your body would be afflicted with a curse that dissolved everything it touched, requiring Dispel Curse to heal.

She really wasn't someone you wanted to make an enemy of.

From there, I lost count of how many floors I passed through.

"Yuika!"

Eventually I found Yuika, driven back into a corner. A colossal humanoid rock was closing in on her.

Or perhaps I should say she was facing certain doom.

I headed straight toward her with all the strength I could muster. Nevertheless, the creature cruelly swung down its stone hand.

Its fist closed in on Yuika, rapidly getting closer and closer.

My thoughts moved in the worst direction. I might already have been too late. No, I could reach her just in time. No, wait, I wouldn't make it.

No, I would *make* myself get there in time.

That's exactly when it happened—the stone colossus's fist slowed down.

For some reason, it was now moving in slow motion. Maybe it was all the adrenaline pumping through me. Or maybe something had caught the creature's attention, and its fist had simply lost speed as a result.

No, no, no—I didn't have the time to think about it. If time had slowed down, then this was my chance. I needed to run over to the stone monster now. All I could do was run.

Run!

A roar loud enough to split one's ears echoed through the area.

It took me by surprise. I didn't think I would make it in time. Maybe it was because my Adrenaline Rush activated.

Putting my power behind my Third Hand, I punched the monster, then unsheathed my blade, continuing to pummel it with my Fourth Hand as I spun around.

Although a noise like stone being smashed with a colossal hammer rang out, I hadn't been able to cut it at all. But I had succeeded in dampening its momentum. The stone humanoid went flying back to the wall.

Unfortunately, it immediately got back on its feet, as though it hadn't been damaged in the slightest.

I turned my sights to Yuika. She could only look back at me in utter befuddlement, barely able to vocalize the words written so clearly on her face.

"……Taki…oto?"

Her body was a painful sight to behold. It was red and swollen in places. She had cuts. Her clothes were in tatters. Her panties were white yet again. She had been beaten up without being able to put up much of a fight.

This monster had driven Yuika against a wall. She'd probably given up hope.

I wanted to put her mind at ease. That was why I spoke to her with a smile.

"What'd I tell you? I'll come flying to the rescue."

Chapter 9 — Yuika Hijiri

—*Yuika's Perspective*—

When I came to, I found myself alone in a world of pitch black, floating feebly on the surface of water.

I didn't understand how I had ended up like this. But a part of me knew things would end up this way.

I could hear the voice of a young girl. When I turned to look, I saw she was wearing a straw hat and running with plenty of energy in her step.

Upon closer inspection, the girl was me. My younger self. The more I stared at her face and hairstyle, the more she resembled me. As I gazed at her, something my father had once told me suddenly popped into my head.

"*You look just like your mother.*"

Apparently, I closely resembled her.

However, she had been dead for as long as I could remember, so I didn't know much about her. There were pictures of her left behind, though, and the women I saw in them was beautiful. More than that, she looked incredibly kind.

The photo that really stuck in my brain was a picture of her in a field of sunflowers. My mother wore a straw hat on her head and a smile on her face that rivaled the beauty of the foliage. She looked like me, just as my father had said.

"*Your mother was an incredible person.*"

Father would always say this to me.

She excelled at any sport she played and was extremely gifted at using holy magic. In fact, my mother had first met my father when she healed an injury of his.

I had apparently inherited a lot from her, as I proved adept with holy magic and healing magic from a young age. Father would praise my talents, yet simultaneously insist that I shouldn't show my holy magic to strangers.

I remembered, despite my young age, asking him why.

At the time, Father said something along the lines of, "You might be taken by bad people if you do," I think. But what stood out to me more was an image of him drinking, holding his head in his hands and muttering, "What in the world am I going to do?" It was burned into my brain.

Perhaps because I had so many things I needed to do, or because I had so many things I needed to think about, I was wiser than other kids my age. I had been ostracized by other children for a portion of my life, too, so I was more sensitive to the feelings of those around me. This period was to blame for why I became someone who strives to be on friendly terms with everyone.

My father had moved us from my mother's homeland of Leggenze to his homeland of Wakoku not only because of her death, but also out of concern for me. Thanks to this move, I stopped being bullied and was able to make friends. That was when my father started talking about remarrying.

The first time I met my big brother was just before he brought up getting married again...when I was ten years old.

He'd been even calmer and quieter back then than he was now; he could use all kinds of magic; he had a sweet tooth. But above all else, he was kind. That was why I always ended up asking him to do stuff for me.

Not that he was without his shortcomings; he was bad at expressing himself, was easily influenced by other people, and was incapable of refusing my requests.

I didn't have any complaints about my new mother, either.

She treated me just like her own child, sometimes harshly, other times kindly, but always with love. Since she was skilled at using magic herself, she would occasionally teach it to Iori and me.

My brother would absorb everything thrown at him like a sponge, so I desperately practiced my own magic to make sure he didn't get the better of me.

All in all, our days had been happy.

▶ Chapter 9: Yuika Hijiri

And then I was kidnapped.

I could vividly remember everything that happened. I found myself taken by the followers of the Church of the Malevolent God to be a sacrifice.

The followers of the Malevolent God had been gathering up users of holy magic, so they must have conspired to kidnap me after noticing my talent for it.

My big brother had been with me at the time and tried to shield me. Nevertheless, my abductor had kicked him aside and dragged me off with him.

There were several other people besides myself at the place where he brought me. The oldest ones looked to be in their thirties, while the youngest were even younger than me. A girl who was a bit older than me cheered me up.

It'll be okay. Help is on the way. Just wait. It was my first time meeting her, yet I felt almost certain that our paths had crossed before.

I remember feeling really anxious when I heard one of the others crying. Their feelings of dread must have been contagious, because soon another person started bawling, then another, and another.

Right when I was on the verge of shedding tears of my own, the older girl placed her hand on my head and said something to me.

She divined my future for me. I was going to be saved. I was bound to experience a lot of pain in the future. But I was going to be okay.

Believe and search for hope. If I did that, I was sure to see the light ahead.

Hearing her say all this, I felt comforted.

After that, we were made to sit in a large magical circle.

Then the Malevolent Gods' followers invoked their spell, and the magic circle below us activated. I grew sleepy as I felt power rapidly drain from me.

I can vaguely remember what happened in that moment.

It wasn't painful. I thought I'd simply close my eyes and drift into death. I'd mentally prepared myself for it, too. But, despite waiting and waiting, death never came for me.

It was then, at that moment, that I was enveloped in a giant hand.

At that point, my drowsiness had reached its limit, so I didn't remember much of what happened after that.

The only thing I could recall was someone with a large, attractive back saying, "What did I tell you?"

When I came to my senses, I saw my big brother and stepmom crying loudly before my eyes.

My brother had tried to come save me but was ultimately unable to do anything. He'd almost gotten killed before a battlemage saved him.

He looked up to that battlemage ever since and put all his efforts into studying magic and the sword.

I also started learning martial arts, in part so I could protect myself, but also because I didn't want Iori to beat me at something. I hated losing, so I practiced relentlessly.

My kidnapping must have caused him to push himself during training.

I had been kidnapped... Kidnapped...............?!

Something wearing a uniform. A hand reaching toward me. A magic circle. Was I......?

"Ngh?!"

I woke up. My back was killing me.

I tried to sit up, but things didn't go very smoothly. Intense pain shot through my arms and stomach, keeping me from moving properly.

Wincing through the pain, I forced myself up and looked around.

I appeared to be in some sort of library. It wasn't the library at the Academy, though. I was lying on the floor.

My clothes were ripped on part of my right arm and stomach, and blood was flowing from lacerations, as though both areas had gotten caught on something.

While I incanted healing magic, I stared ahead.

Walking away from me was a nonhuman being dressed in the Academy uniform.

I thought back to the blow I'd felt on my back. Did that mean this thing had carried me all the way here before tossing me to the ground?

As I watched them walk off, I suddenly recalled everything that had happened up until that point.

Right. That thing had just dragged me into a teleportation circle. And then......it brought me here.

I stared hard at the creature, which was growing distant. Its silhouette was similar to that of a beastfolk or human, but it had a goat-like face, a snake tail, and long, crinkled claws growing from its hands. From its claws, I saw drops of scarlet blood falling to the floor.

A demon, plain as day.

There was a book floating in front of the demon, and on the other side of the book was a black sphere hovering in the air. Below the black sphere was a large magic circle that glowed and crackled.

The demon slowly brought its blood-soaked claws up to the floating book.

With a deafening screech, the barrier between it and the book began to tear apart. Then it stabbed its claw through the pages.

Right as the book was pierced through, the magic circle below the black orb crackled loudly, like surging electricity, and disappeared.

Oh, so that book must have been the seal for that orb.

The black sphere fell to the floor with a thud.

Then it suddenly started to wobble, slowly transforming into an oval shape.

Finished casting my healing magic, I stared at the unknown object, and the thoughts urging me to escape grew louder in my mind.

I activated my mana to swiftly scan my surroundings. I was a fair distance from the exit to the corridor. I didn't have anything on me, either.

The demon suddenly turned back my way.

"So you came to, huh?" it said, smirking wickedly as it closed in on where I was. "I searched long and hard for you. It surprised me when you disappeared after I tried to scare you, but that also convinced me you were what I was looking for. Clearly it was worth crossing through so many countries to get this far."

Hearing this, I thought back to the incident at Susano Martial Arts Academy. This thing must have been my stalker.

"Well then, let's head to the next seal, shall we?" it continued, but as it closed in on me, I backed away. I didn't really know what that meant, but I wasn't going to find out.

"You'd do best to listen to what I say. You don't want to get hurt, do you?"

Would I be able to escape? While I had found what looked like a corridor, it was still far away.

My gauntlets……were gone at the moment. I would've had a bit more power at my disposal if they were still with me, but wishing for something I didn't have wasn't going to get me anywhere.

Suddenly, I felt a large amount of mana from behind the demon, and I shifted my focus toward it.

The demon appeared to feel the same thing and turned around.

"Ugaugh!"

Just then, it was impaled by sharpened ice. It wasn't a single piece of ice, either. Close to ten shards were flying toward the two of us.

I immediately dodged the icicles using the demon as a shield. It shouted something, but after four of the shards had lodged themselves inside its body, it dissolved into magic particles.

I didn't have a clue what was going on, but I did know I was in big trouble.

I could try to flee, but the exit was still a ways off. And if more magic was fired my way while I turned my back to run, I'd become target practice for the caster.

So was I supposed to fight?

I activated my mana and used enhancement magic on myself. Then, turning to face the slime-looking monster that had begun an incantation of its own, I broke into a sprint.

Once I stepped into range, I delivered an uppercut to it with my enhanced fist. Its body launched into the air, and I sent out a straight thrust forward.

A beautiful direct hit. That's what I thought, at least.

I felt the blow connect, and I watched its body go flying.

"All right……… Wait, what?"

When the creature hit the floor, it bounced straight up, then began to squish and transform in midair. It morphed itself into the shape of a beast before touching down on the ground again.

A magic circle immediately materialized, and from it, four green blades came flying toward me.

"Nhg!"

I dodged them by a hairsbreadth, but one of the blades got my uniform, tearing it in a way Takioto would've definitely enjoyed seeing.

"Uh, are you serious?"

I stared at the beast in bewilderment. My attack had been ineffective—and had caused it to transform? I couldn't help feeling nauseous as I looked at the thing, now standing firm on its four legs.

What the hell was this thing?

I wanted an answer. It was all so bizarre. Just a second ago, this thing had been a blob. Yet now it had perfectly transformed into some kind of wolf creature. It moved in a totally different way, too, and it closely observed me as though it were a predatory feline.

The creature seemed to vanish for an instant, but that was only because it had leapt to the side. Then it closed in at a speed unlike any I had witnessed before, its claws outspread toward me.

"Whoa, whoa!"

Another close call. It scratched a single line across my thigh with its sharp claws, but that was it. The wound wasn't enough to slow me down.

I kicked it in exchange, but that only caused the phenomenon from earlier to repeat.

"I definitely can feel my hit connect, so could someone tell me why it seems like I'm not doing anything here?"

I immediately opened up space between myself and the beast, watching it go flying.

It really seemed like my attacks hadn't done anything in the slightest. The creature quickly collapsed its shape and transformed into a lizard this time. Though it looked big enough to swallow a human whole, it moved a little slower than its wolf form.

It glared me down and slowly opened its mouth. Inside its maw were not bodily fluids, but a slowly rotating magic circle.

A stream of fireballs came flying from its mouth, and I jumped sideways just in the nick of time. I managed to dodge the flames since I had reacted immediately, but I accomplished nothing beyond that.

I let the lizard get in close, then managed to evade its incoming bite, only to be sent flying.

"Huh?"

All of a sudden, I was sprawled out on the floor.

The world around me was spinning, like my balance had been thrown out of whack. I couldn't see where my opponent was.

"Oooh, it must've been the tail."

It had probably struck me with its tail from my blind spot. I thought my brains were spilling out of my ears for a moment there.

It was a little late to realize it after it already hit me, but I clearly couldn't afford to get hit by its tail swipe.

What I thought was the lizard again opening its mouth wide was instead the signal for another slow transformation. This time, the creature came out looking like a golem. It slowly advanced toward me, loud thuds echoing with each step.

I was starting to catch onto my enemy's quirks.

It could transform itself into a number of different forms, and each one of those forms had its own unique characteristics. The wolf form had speed, the lizard was balanced, the slime had its magic and flexibility, while now, the golem form…

"Probably power, huh…… I gotta split."

My mind was running on all cylinders, and I knew what I needed to do. The problem was my body wouldn't keep up with it.

I couldn't get up.

When I tried, I lost my balance and flopped back onto my butt. The golem loomed over me, and my brain kicked into overdrive.

I bet I'm going to die here.

Just as that thought crossed my mind, a few images popped into my head.

Takioto.

I'd called him to meet with me but ended up ditching him.

For some reason, I always felt super secure when he was around.

Why was that?

I'd never even planned on bringing up the stalker incident, but then blabbed all about it to him anyway.

Dad, Mom.

I wasn't able to repay you for anything. Even after all the trouble I caused you both.

Between the bullying and the move.

The truth is, Dad, I had seen you drinking late at night, crying to yourself, a bunch of times before.

I wish I could've done something to show how much I care about you both, but I'm sorry I couldn't.

I made you worried sick when I was kidnapped, Mom.

I still remember how very warm your hug felt when you wrapped

▶ Chapter 9: Yuika Hijiri

your arms around me and Iori. We talked about going to a hot spring together, and now I wished we had gone sooner.

Big brother.
I've caused you a lot of trouble, haven't I?
Nothing but nonstop headaches, right?
I mean, you always did whatever I asked, shrugging it off with an "Okay, fine, I guess" whenever I needed to rely on you.
I had already burdened Dad plenty, so I couldn't have him spoil me. That was why I ended up depending on your kindness instead. I'm so, so grateful for that.
But you still haven't won a single fight against me, have you? It seems like you've built up a remarkable amount of strength lately, but I guess I'll be bowing out before you have a chance to claim victory. Sorry about that.

Slowly, the golem's fist descended on me. Welp, death was—
A massive clang echoed through the area. Yet the fist still hadn't reached me. Not only that, but the golem itself was completely gone.
Standing there in its stead was a boy with his back to me, wrapped up in a large red stole.
His back was super badass and super attractive.
He turned his face to me and smiled.
"What'd I tell you? I'll come flying to the rescue."

She looked almost like a small child staring blankly up in confusion. Yuika's expression—eyes wide, mouth half open, and completely dumbstruck—was a little bit silly, but also kind of cute.
Her eyes were moving every which way, and a tear was tracing a line down her cheek. Yuika didn't bother wiping it off as she stared at me.
"This can't be real…… Am I hallucinating or something?"
"I'm the real deal. You think there's anyone else out there with good looks like these?"
Pointing my thumb at myself, I gave her a wink, channeling Minister Benito. I made the hammy comment to try bringing some levity to the situation at hand, but Yuika seemed to be really confused, so she

didn't follow up with a retort of her own. Now I just seemed like a cringy loser.

"Why..."

"Why? C'mon, what kinda question is that?"

I opened my stole and lifted her up with my empty hands, bridal style.

Behind me, the Black Magic Stone, now shifted into its slime form, had just finished invoking its spell.

Judging from the number of ice blades that were flying toward me, it looked to be the mid-level magic spell, Icicle Rain.

"Take this, for example."

I quickly opened my Third Hand and deflected the icy blades as I moved.

"*Eeyah!* Your friend's been kidnapped. If that happens, it's pretty obvious what you gotta do, right?"

Yukine had used this magic on me plenty of times before. Generally, the shards would only be fired in a straight line from where the spell was cast, and the spell could be maintained to keep firing ice in succession. I could stay where we were and keep blocking them, but I could also move in an arc away from the spell's origin point.

The shards were easy to evade when I knew they were coming.

Once I slipped out of the attack range, I threw a sigiled wind stone as payback.

The blades of wind brought forth by the stone scored a direct hit on the Magic Stone Muck, and it transformed its body, squirming in agony and hissing loudly.

Yuika stared blankly at the Magic Stone Muck writhing in pain.

"Sorry 'bout picking you up like that."

"Oh no, um, thank you."

Though it wasn't by much, Yuika looked like she was feeling a bit better. I blocked the incoming stone projectiles with my stole. They must have been from the mid-level earth spell, Stalactite Machine Gun.

I watched as Yuika dodged the incoming attack on her own two feet this time, and I realized she had calmed herself down a bit.

When the monster's attack ended, Yuika suddenly muttered quietly:

"Why...did you come?" She sounded like she was on the verge of tears. "I'm really, really happy that you've come for me. But... Please get out of here. We can't beat that thing," she said, wringing the words

out of her mouth. "It's really strong. It nullified all my attacks, and they didn't seem to have any effect at all."

In response to Yuika's fainthearted protest, I let out an exaggerated guffaw.

"C'mon now, that's not the Yuika I know. Listen, you're supposed to tell me something like, 'I never even asked for your help, I was about to bring it down myself,' or 'Step aside, big brother! You can't kill this thing!' That sorta stuff."

"...I'm not really *trying* to come off like I'm not honest with my feelings, or that I've got a sick, unhealthy obsession with Iori or anything. Besides, you're not even my brother to begin with, Takioto."

"Yuika, you're still all confused. Take a deep breath and think hard. I'm your big brother Iori's best friend, right? So, I'm basically your brother, too. Your brother in spirit."

"......Excuse me? You're not making any sense—it seems like *you're* the one who could use some deep breaths. Take a look at the situation we're in."

She maaaay have had a point. For the time being, I blocked the fireballs flying at us with my stole while we both took deep breaths.

Recollecting my thoughts for a moment, the first thing that came to mind was—

"Let's wrap this up fast and go grab some food or something. I guess with what happened yesterday, it can be my treat."

"So you really aren't looking at the present situation we're in at all, then?"

"No, no, I can see what's going on here. Just think about it. A puny-looking enemy going up against me. That's basically a guaranteed victory, right? Plus, I've got you with me. No way we can lose."

"But......"

"No buts about it. You seem to think you haven't damaged this thing at all, but that's not actually true. It's feeling the pain all right. Promise."

"Huh?"

"Look."

I changed the elemental enchanting my stole to water. Leaving Yuika behind, I kicked off against the ground toward the Magic Stone Muck.

The creature shifted into its lizard form, opening its maw to launch fireballs at me as I closed in. I broke through its front guard with my stole, then blocked a blow from its tail with my Third Hand. Then, standing right in front of it, I slammed my Fourth Hand right into its side, the look Yuika had worn on her face moments earlier on my mind.

"How about that, huh?!"

The Muck went flying, squirming its body around in a big mush and letting out a hiss.

"Wh-why?"

I could hear Yuika's cry of confusion. I stood in front of her, then repelled the stone projectiles the Magic Stone Muck's newly shape-shifted form sent our way.

"This monster's a huge pain in the ass to defeat, and despite what it looks like, it's a type of slime."

"That's a *slime*?! Wait, but why do you know that?"

Of course I would know. There was a time when I was basically a walking Magical★Explorer database. I wanted to explain and comment on things so much that it would weird people out. However.

"As much as I'd like to explain everything, now's not the time. I'll be brief," I said before looking over to see what the monster was doing. Its next spell hadn't come yet.

"Every time this thing changes forms, its elemental weakness changes with it. If you don't hit its weakness, it's hard to deal a lot of damage to it. Thing is, it's got enough stamina that you'd never be able to fully whittle it down without hitting it where it hurts."

"So basically, you're saying we need to attack it with its elemental weakness?"

"That's right. So it's vital to figure out what that weakness is."

Trying to take it on without knowing about any of this would definitely end up being a total disaster.

"But how exactly are we supposed to figure that out...... Wait."

"That's right, it's actually pretty easy to distinguish them. You can use the shape it's transformed into or the magic it uses to determine which element to deploy against it."

Its fire-wielding lizard form was weak to water, its water-wielding slime form was vulnerable to wind, its wind magic–wielding form struggled against earth, and its earth-wielding golem form was trounced by fire.

After hearing this, Yuika was quick to act. She enveloped her arm in fire, dashed at the monster, still in its slime form, and shoved her fist into the magic circle right on the verge of activation.

The fist directly hit the Magic Stone Muck as it burst through the shattered magic circle. Watching the Magic Stone Muck again let out a hiss as it writhed in pain, Yuika tried to stab her fist into the monster again, but by then it had already changed shape and dodged her attack.

I sized up its new form, swapped out my stole's enchantment, and smacked it hard. I missed just slightly, and took some damage myself, but Yuika used her healing magic to help me recover from the wound.

"Things would be nice and easy if they kept up like this."

After we repeated the same approach over and over again and a pattern to victory appeared to emerge, it happened—

It transformed into a shape that we hadn't seen it use yet.

It looked like a skinny golem. Its body was humanoid-shaped, but it had curled horns on its head and black wings sprouting from its back. To top all of this off, it held a pitch-black longsword in its right hand.

"Takioto, what is its weakness supposed to be this time?!" Yuika shouted, standing a bit removed from my current location.

At the same moment, the Magic Stone Muck made its move. Yup, I could tell just from the mana it was enveloped in. This was bad news, all right. One side wasn't going to be enough. I needed to layer both the right and left sides of my stole together in order to block its next attack.

The creature brought down its sword. I spread my Third and Fourth Hands out in front of me. The area shook with a deafening roar.

It was just as loud as the rumble Minister Benito had produced when he'd blocked the titan's attack earlier.

"Its weakness......is everything but dark magic."

The Magic Stone Muck's attack sent a shock through my body. Just as I considered what we would do next, I could see a foot come into view.

Well, crap. A ridiculously fast kick was coming my way...

"*Gwaugh!*"

"Takioto?!"

Although I instantly brought up my arms in a defensive position, the power behind the kick was tremendous.

Yuika's healing magic immediately flew toward me. Boy, was I seriously grateful she was here. The force of the blow had convinced me the kick would break my arms and send my organs flying in all directions.

It appeared that blood was indeed flying out of me, though.

"Be careful, Yuika. That demon form is its enraged mode; in exchange for gaining a bunch more weaknesses, its abilities skyrocket."

The creature was fighting with its back up against a wall. Without any other options, it had thrown aside any defenses and shifted all its power into offense.

Now it seemed to be targeting Yuika and her healing magic. It turned to her and swung its sword down. Yuika sidestepped and barely managed to dodge the attack, but she couldn't keep dodging it forever.

I quickly got in between the two of them and parried the monster's strike.

The offensive power it wielded wasn't to be underestimated. If I took its sword head-on, I was bound to get sliced clean in two.

"Takioto, you said this thing seemed weak, right? Mind telling me what about this thing's weak?!"

Looked like the jig was up. Best to make things clear. Our opponent was far beyond the two of us. Why did we have to fight a mid-game enemy like this right here, right now, anyway?

If I was by myself, I would've booked it, no questions asked. Why would I need to go out of my way to square off against a powerful foe like this? Did I really want its piddling amount of experience points and its wholly replaceable item drops enough to jump into this super risky scenario? Nope, not in the slightest.

But when I'd heard Yuika was there, everything changed.

I handled its attack. I dealt with the next one, too. Then, looking for an opening, I weaved in blows of my own.

The Magic Stone Muck's abilities were currently on par with Icarus's rage mode. Potentially even stronger.

Would I really be able to beat an enemy like that? I mean, it was practically a given, wasn't it? After all, right now—

"You didn't forget about me, did you?! You left yourself wide open!"

I wasn't alone.

If I got hit with an attack, Yuika would heal me. If Yuika got herself in trouble, I'd defend her. We worked in tandem, waiting for the right timing.

Our breathing was so in sync, it was like I had another version of myself at my side.

I didn't think we'd lose at all.

The Magic Stone Muck seemed to have run out of patience, as it now swung its sword of darkness in large arcs toward us. However, Yuika's uppercut was able to stop it in its tracks. Then she shouted to me.

"Takioto!"

"Leave it to me!"

The Magic Stone Muck's arms were dangling from Yuika's strike as it flew up into the air. Both guarding and dodging were impossible.

I couldn't let this chance slip.

Jumping out in front of Yuika, I took one more step forward. Then I drew my katana, unleashing all the power I had stored up.

I could see the line telling me where I needed to slice.

After that, I simply traced it with a flash of steel.

Watching the monster slowly dissolve into magic particles, Yuika spoke to me.

"Hey, Takioto."

"What is it?"

"Thanks for everything today. And…"

"And?"

She flashed a smile my way.

"I'm gonna order everything off the menu, top to bottom. I hope you're ready for it," she said, a wide smile stretching across her whole face.

Yuika was cute when she was playing the fool, sure, but she was the cutest of all when she wore a smile on her face.

Chapter 10 — Her Name Was Gabby, Gabriella Evangelista

After crushing the Magic Stone Muck, it didn't take long to meet up with Shion and Minister Benito. It seemed like they caught the end of our fight, and they sang our praises for how well we'd handled the monster.

The compliments were nice, sure, but if they really had been there, I wished they would've joined in to help. I didn't say anything like that, of course, and gave them a proper thank-you instead. However, Minister Benito flashed a suggestive smile my way and told me, "Let me be the first to apologize. Sorry in advance." I had no clue what he meant.

Shion also seemed to have taken quite a liking to Yuika, and the two agreed to meet up later.

From there, Yuika and I didn't grab a bite to eat or anything like that. She, Shion, Minister Benito, and I were all totally spent. Our stamina was at its limits by the time we finished explaining everything to Sis and everyone else who was waiting outside the dungeon for us.

Unable to bear the thought of Yuika going back to the dorm right after being kidnapped, Marino insisted that she stay at her place.

Then we ate and conked out. The sun was already high in the sky by the time we woke up.

Nanami seemed to resent me for going off into a dungeon to save Yuika without her, grumbling that "I wasn't worried about you at all or anything, Master, nope, not one bit" and "You've got a lot of nerve leaving me behind, you know." I tripped up trying to quip back at her with my sluggish, sleep-addled brain.

I wanted to ask her what the hell she was putting me through first thing in the morning, but I resigned myself to throwing in the towel.

I heard that Nanami had actually been very worried and had nearly charged after us into the dungeon by herself.

I went down the stairs into the living room and found Yuika there, having just woken up herself.

Her hair was down, and she was rubbing her eyes, still looking very sleepy.

Once we had finished getting dressed for the day, it was already past noon, and Yuika generously reminded me about my promise to treat her to a meal. Right now? My reluctance to do this chore must have shown on my face.

But once the word *treadmill* left her mouth, the only response I could give was a hearty "I'd love to."

"Whoooa! This is suuuuper delish, Takioto!"

Sitting below a radiantly shining sun, Yuika and I enjoyed an elegant lunch on the open patio of a restaurant after I'd narrowly prevented her from actually ordering one of everything on the menu.

"I mean, skipping school to get treated to lunch by yours truly? Obviously that's gonna taste good."

"I'm not cutting class! This doesn't count!" Yuika said as she brought some spaghetti to her lips.

Indeed, Marino told us she would make an exception and mark us as present today, so we weren't really skipping. Given that we were enjoying lunch like this while everyone else was in the middle of their school day, though, the outing did have a forbidden thrill to it.

We enjoyed a coffee together after finishing our meal. Just then, Yuika spoke up in an earnest tone.

"Takioto... Thank you."

"No problem. If your stomach's happy, then I'm happy."

I gathered what she actually meant from her frown, but I brushed it aside with my reply. I didn't particularly want her worrying about the incident anyway. Besides, hearing her thank me to my face like this made me feel a bit bashful.

"No, no, no, that's not what I'm talking about."

Nevertheless, Yuika was keen on making sure I knew what she was talking about.

"I'm thanking you for coming to my rescue, of course. You're just playing dumb, aren't you?"

▶ Chapter 10: Her Name Was Gabby, Gabriella Evangelista   143

I actively averted my eyes, prompting a weak smile from Yuika.
"I really thought I was going to die back there. My dad, my stepmom, and my big brother's faces all flashed before my eyes. There was still so much I wanted to accomplish, that I wasn't going to be able to...... I really didn't want to go out like that. So, thank you."
"......C'mon, don't even worry about it."
"I am worrying about it, though. Of course I am! How could I possibly not have it on my mind? And well, with that said..."
"What?"
"I want you to call for my help if you're the one in trouble next time, Takioto. I'll be there for you."
"You sure you wanna say that? Some of the students at the Academy think I'm a bit of a maniac, and they're not wrong, you know. I'm gonna have you tagging along with me to trek through some super dangerous dungeons."
"Yup, I'll be there. If I can help, anyway. Besides, if something happens...," she said, looking at me with upturned doe eyes.
"You'll be there to protect me, won't you?"
"......'Course I will."
The smile on her face was a bit different than usual. It was slightly stilted, somewhat awkward and embarrassed.
"Hey, Takioto?"
"What's up?"
"Um, well, it's a little bit embarrassing to say this, but... When you showed up to save me, your back—"
"Kouuuuuusukeeeeeee Taaaaaaaakiiiiiioooooootooooo!"
Right as I heard the shout drown out Yuika's next words, a girl suddenly charged into the restaurant like a hurricane.
"You shan't be getting away this time! Where is Takioto Kousuke?! You, spit it out!"
I heard a commotion coming from inside.
Welp, this was bad news. For some reason, this girl was so angry she was spewing like a volcano. But why? Seriously, what in the world was *Gabby* doing here?
"Yuika...... Let's get out of here."
Urging on Yuika, who was taken aback by the ranting and raving voice from within, I left money on the table for the bill.
Then I got up from my chair and crouched down low in an attempt

to slip away unnoticed. However, before we could make our escape, Gabby exited the restaurant.

"I-I've found you now! Finally, *finally*, I've got you noooow!"

Yuika turned directly toward the source of the voice. I didn't need to look to know who it was. Her voice was more than enough of a giveaway. What was with her timing, though? Actually, it may have been more accurate to say this encounter was long overdue.

I had suspected she would swing by, to be honest. About as confident in my prediction as I was confident that a childhood-friend heroine in an eroge still had her virginity intact.

I followed Yuika's lead and turned around—sure enough, there she was.

Her blond hair was even yellower than Ludie's. It was styled in a very unique way, curled so tight it resembled drills.

Her body was trembling slightly, perhaps out of lingering anger.

"You're always hiding from me! Always! Even now, I find you lying low in this place!"

"I mean, we're on a patio, so I don't think you can say he was hiding..."

Though Yuika's rebuttal was sound, Gabby obviously ignored it entirely. Aww. That was so very much like her, too.

If you asked me whether I liked her or not, my answer would be that she was one of my wives. No matter what game it was, I loved any and all haughty rich girl characters like her. A certain Elder Sister game about cross-dressing to attend a private girls' academy was likely the source of these feelings.

"*Uuugh*, you're never on campus when I try to go see you...... Always absent, always gone! I heard that you had come to campus and I tried visiting your class, but you still weren't there!"

I had to apologize for that one. While I already avoided coming to school to begin with, I had planned on avoiding Gabby as much as possible as I went about my business—at least until Minister Benito finished smoothing things over for me. Wait, I had totally forgotten to ask Minister Benito to do that, hadn't I?

Still, Gabby was getting into stalker territory here, wasn't she?

"Being top of the class without taking a single test... It's ridiculous...!"

Well, that was ultimately how the comprehensive scoring system worked, so there wasn't really much I could do about that.

"Not only that, but joining the Ceremonial Committee right after taking top of the class, too! You obviously used some underhanded trickery to worm your way in there—I just know it!"

I couldn't quite place it, but maybe it was because I knew she'd be coming to see me. Instead of feeling any stress from the—honestly—unquestionably false accusations she was leveling at me, my mind was at peace. Her caustic language felt nice and cozy. This was the Gabby I knew and loved.

"And of all things, even my brother... *Gaaah*! Ab-so-lutely outrageous! You've done just about everything to infuriate me, haven't you?!"

...Aha, so Minister Benito must've done something, then. He'd gone and made her even more upset. I could already imagine the *Whoops sorry, lol* message I'd be getting from him later.

"Let me be perfectly clear... I absolutely shall not tolerate any of this!"

"I mean, I didn't cheat or anything..."

"Liar!"

Welp, this isn't getting anywhere, I thought, inwardly sighing as I glanced from the enraged girl in front of me to Yuika.

Her normal smile had disappeared, and she now looked flabbergasted instead. Gabby was...intense, let's say...so I didn't really blame her.

.........All that said, this was a pretty funny situation.

Me, Kousuke Takioto, member of the Ceremonial Committee.

Minister Benito's younger sister and potential future Ceremonial Committee member, Gabby.

Finally, while it did depend on certain events, a heroine who could potentially join any of the Three Committees, as well as Iori Hijiri's younger stepsister, Yuika Hijiri.

Who would have thought all these Ceremonial Committee–related characters would come together like this?

"Kousuke Takioto! I, Gabriella Evangelista, demand you duel me fair and square!!"

As I considered how exactly I was going to respond to her, Yuika practically chimed in on my behalf.

"L-let's just calm down here, okay, Ms. Evangelista?"

"Oh, I don't believe we've had the pleasure?"

"Nice to meet you, I'm Yuika Hijiri. I'm not really sure what you're getting at, so I'm just a liiiiittle confused about what's such a big deal here."

"Why, it is *very* simple, I say! That boy there used some cowardly trickery to steal the top rank in the class!"

Well, I had to admit that depending on your perspective, plunging into the dungeon on the day of the test was a bit of an underhanded tactic. Plenty of people who saw what I did reacted by saying, "Wait, since when was that allowed?!"

"Now, now. Sure, it may have been a bit unfair, but can't you just say he exploited a loophole in the rules and let it go? We'll all be challenging the dungeon next time anyway, and I'm sure the class rankings will see a big changeup once that happens. Why don't we let bygones be bygones and look ahead to the next exams?!"

Believe me, I would have loved if that was enough to get her to back off, but this was Gabby we were dealing with.

As far as the next school rankings went, I felt like her rank would only fall even further because of other people coming into prominence. Though, if Gabby worked herself to the bone clearing dungeons and studying for the tests, she might be able to beat me, specifically. I wasn't aiming to be top of the class next time, that was for sure.

From the very beginning, I'd only aimed to get the top rank in class because the Seeds of Possibility and my membership in the Three Committees were pivotal to my plans. Scoring the same rank next time would only award me some items and Tsukuyomi Points.

I could get my hands on much more valuable items inside the dungeons, so it would be a waste of valuable time if I stopped for a week to take some tests.

If I was thinking of stopping my dungeon activities to take exams, I would be better off just taking a break for a few days for a change of pace. All of this would have been much different if I'd joined the Morals Committee or the Student Council, though.

"Well, *obvious*ly I shall be taking the top spot next time."

A classic Gabby line. I couldn't get enough of her conceited side. And the fact that she usually ended up losing out anyway was the icing on the cake.

While I felt bad for Gabby, fresh off her declaration that she'd earn the top rank in our class, I estimated Ludie would be the one to snag that honor next time. Her, or someone else who went to clear dungeons with me while also taking the test seriously enough to study.

Would Iori and the others come next? Nanami could probably snag the top spot in class if she took things seriously, but if I was skipping out on the tests, she'd be right there alongside me.

Ultimately, I could imagine her saying she didn't even care if she graduated or not.

That fact was, she did earnestly tell me things like, "My employment is eternally with you, Master." She was so unbelievably dependable, I really hoped it would play out like that, too.

"Mind you, I shan't forgive your cheating! But even worse than that, even worse, I say!"

She vigorously pointed the parasol in her hand at me.

"I shall never, I say, N-E-V-E-R, forgive your schemes to win over my brother and use him for your nefarious tricks!"

...From what I was hearing here, it sounded like Minister Benito had ended up pissing her off. In the game, a few of her events happen after a single word of his sets her on a rampage, so I assumed something similar was at play here. She had a pretty severe brother complex—not that Yuika was any better.

As I resigned myself to the situation, Yuika quietly whispered into my ear.

"Takioto, are you plotting something?"

"Like hell I am. Let me ask you, do I look like a guy with a hidden agenda up his sleeve?"

That wasn't to say I hadn't done any thinking about how I would gain notoriety as a Ceremonial Committee member. Minister Benito had mentioned pitching in to help me out, but this was something that all the members decided on together. Above all else, I hadn't once thought about taking advantage of Minister Benito in the slightest.

"Yuika Hijiri, was it? Don't hang around a cowardly rogue like him. It shall only serve to bring you down to his level. You still have time to save yourself," Gabby said, prompting a tilt of Yuika's head.

"Takioto? A coward? I don't know… He's very gentlemanly and strong. More importantly, he's kind and friendly, too," Yuika replied before grabbing my arm and smiling. Then she looked up at me and winked.

Jeez, she was so adorable. And Iori got to hear her call him big brother?

▶ Chapter 10: Her Name Was Gabby, Gabriella Evangelista   149

If the world got flipped upside down, then maybe, just maybe, she would start calling *me* big brother instead...

Gabby looked at my face and trembled. It wasn't long before she couldn't hold herself back anymore and started cackling.

"*P-pfft*. Oh my, how unbecoming, forgive me. I didn't mean to burst out laughing like that, it's just, 'g-gentlemanly,' *p-pffft*, 'gentlemanly,' is he?"

Putting the fact that Yuika had called me "strong" and "kind" aside for a second, I was confident about being a gentleman. As long as you slapped a "pervert" right after it, that was.

But boy, was I deep in it now. An absolute goner. Gabby was so, so, cute. I wished that maybe some huge miracle, like the earth and sea swapping places, would happen so I could hear her call me big brother instead.

"E-even for a joke, that's...*tee-hee-hee*...just too far. *Pfft, hee-hee-hee*, if someone like *him* looks like a gentleman to you, why, I almost feel sorry for what your life must have been like up until now, Yuika."

I only heard her response because she had latched onto my arm.

"Excuse me?" she breathed out quietly.

Then she swiftly strengthened her grip.

I focused all my senses on my arm, feeling something small, yet soft, with just the slightest bit of firmness...... Ow, ow, ow, ow, ow, ow, ow, ow!

"Y-Yuika? Calm down, you gotta stay calm."

Despite my quiet pleading, Yuika didn't move an inch as she locked eyes on Gabby, who was buckling with laughter. Just then, Yuika twisted her lips into a devious smile.

"Um, well, soooo, first off, do you even *know* the truth about the Ceremonial Committee or...?"

Yiiiikes! Uh, Yuika? Your voice was awfully scary there.

"Why, my big brother is the Ceremonial Minister, you know. Of course I know all about it! Yes, if anyone should be called a gentleman, why, it is my big brother Benito!"

"Oh, is that so, hmmm? So that must mean you've realized it, right? There's a whole bunch of stuff that the Ceremonial Committee can't talk about."

"Don't be absurd. Aren't you aware that I'm a certified top student in our class? I'm practically an informal member of the Three Committees already. As such, I have been privy to many things that you must *certainly* be in the dark about."

The way she'd casually claimed to be the top of her class was yet another aspect of Gabby to love.

"First of all, my big brother would never hide something from me. And yet, not only did he hesitate to discuss anything about Kousuke Takioto, but he even tried to cover for his cowardice when I complained about his trickery! It's clear Kousuke did something dreadful to my dear brother. There's no mistaking it!"

"Oh wooooow, are you sure maybe he wasn't hesitating to say anything because he was too creeped out by that gross brother complex of yours?"

Uhhhhhhhhhhhhhhhhhhh?!

"You mentioned your brother is the Ceremonial Minister, right? Seeing you now really lays bare what sort of upbringing he must have had. Looks to me like he should resign immediately and cede his position to Takioto instead."

Hold on a second, Yuika! Wh-why were you riling her up?! I expected Gabby to stir the pot, but I didn't think you'd fight right back! By the way, my arm is really starting to hurt, and your grip's only getting tighter!

"...I won't stand for anyone badmouthing my brother, understand?"

"Aww, don't say that. I'm just calling it how I see it, really. I'm quite surprised, though, Ms. Evangelista, I guess you really have nothing but red beans stuffed in that head of yours, huh? Who would've thought!"

Gaaaaaaaaaaaaaah!

"......I demand an apology."

"Okay. How about you apologize to Takioto first?"

"I have absolutely *no* reason to apologize to *him*."

"Then I guess I don't have any reason to say sorry to you, either! Hmph!"

Hold on a second, what the hell was going on here?! There was clearly mana pouring out of both of their bodies right now! They never exhibit any hostility toward each other in-game at all! Hell, they get pretty friendly with each other over their shared love of big brothers, so what was with all this?!

"...It appears that I have not one but two insects to crush beneath me here. Insects with foul mouths, at that."

"Um, was that supposed to be your own self-introduction? And clearly there's only one insect standing here right now. Is that brain of yours working properly? Oh, I'm so sorry, that must be what it's always like!" Somebody, save me...! Somebody, anybody, do *something* about this mess! And spare some healing magic for my arm while you're at it......

"......I assume you're fully prepared for what comes next?"

"You took the words straight from my mouth. If you apologize now, I might just let you off the hook."

The two stared each other down, sending an electric crackle into the air.

Resigned to it all, I gazed up at the sky. Ahhh, what beautiful weather we were having today.

Chapter 11 (Mystery)

"And that's how things finally turned out."
In the end, Yuika and Gabby agreed to settling things later rather than duking it out on the spot.
"You had it rough, didn't you?"
Marino welcomed me when I came to her room. She must have been in the middle of work, as there were piles of documents on her table. A transparent display showing a magic circle and glyphs of some sort floated in midair.
"Yeah, it was a real stressful afternoon."
Marino handed me a cup of coffee and sat down on her sofa. Then she raised the cup she had made for herself and took a sip.
"Thank you very much. If you insist," I said before taking a sip of my own. The coffee had a sweet aroma to it, like strawberry jam.
Though the bitterness characteristic of coffee spread across my mouth, it quickly faded into a sourness instead.
"This is tasty. Especially the aroma, it's wonderful."
"I'm glad you like it. They're Leggenze beans, a personal favorite of mine. I could share some with you, if you want."
"I'd love that."
"I'll bring them to your room later. Be sure to pay attention to the brew time, okay? Too long or too short and you won't bring out its aroma... Now, is it all right if we get back to why you're here?"
"Yes, please."
"This stays between us, okay? The truth is, I'm pretty busy right now. But since it's my beloved little Kou asking, I stopped working to chat with you. That must score a lot of points, right?"
"If Takioto Points were a thing, this would earn you some, I'd say."
"Oh my ♪," Marino said before bringing both her hands up to her

cheeks and squirming in embarrassment. Very theatrical. She was trying *too* hard. Just how old did she think she was here? It was adorable either way, so obviously, she had scored herself some more points.

"Sorry. So what is it, then?"

"I have something I'd like to talk with you about, Marino."

"Right, right. Sounds like it's pretty serious, too. You always make me brace for the worst when you're polite with me like this."

"Your intuition was correct. And it's quite the major topic at that."

I also thought that she probably wouldn't answer me, or she'd just lie.

"It concerns you, Marino."

"If it's just about my body measurements, I wouldn't mind telling you."

"If you're asking whether I want to know those or not, I'd have to say that I'd like to pretend that I don't care at all, while secretly knowing all about them—but that's got nothing to do with what I'm getting at."

"*Tee-hee-hee*, thanks."

"None of that matters at all. Anyway, there's this huge question I've had on my mind."

It was regarding the character of Marino Hanamura, who is almost never talked about in the original game.

"When I heard Yuika's story, I got this this feeling, like a fish bone stuck in my throat, that something wasn't quite lining up."

"Yuika's story?"

"About why she transferred here. So I asked Ms. Ruija to do some digging into her circumstances."

"...So that explains why she was poking around in things that normally wouldn't have interested anyone."

According to what I heard, transferring into Tsukuyomi Magic Academy was very rare, and there hadn't been any examples of someone coming in right after the start of the new term, either. Then...

"It sounds like you were pretty pushy about recommending Yuika to transfer here, too."

"You know about her, right, Kousuke? How strong she is? How amazing she is?"

"I'm aware. Better than anyone in the Three Committees, better than her friends, and even better than her stepbrother Iori."

I knew things about Yuika that even she hadn't realized.

"Then you get it, right? It'd be a waste of her potential to have a girl

Chapter 11: Mystery

of her skills somewhere like Susano Martial Arts Academy. She'd be a tough opponent during the Inter-Academy Tournament, too. Besides…"

"There was the stalker incident, right?"

"I just wanted to help her, of course."

"I'm sure that you did actually want to help her. But that's just the official reason, isn't it?"

"Oh…?"

Just then, I felt like the look in Marino's eyes had changed.

It might have been a trick of the light. To be honest, her expression was exactly the same as it was a few moments ago. Nevertheless, the air around us had gotten heavier, like the room would bend in on itself to crush me unless I braced myself.

"Ms. Ruija researched the minute details of the arrangement itself, the date, time, and the like. To keep it short and simple, the whole thing played out much more forcefully than one would have expected. Not only that, but you quietly gave her a bodyguard detail until she arrived in town, didn't you?"

"…How do you know about the bodyguards?"

"Sorry, I just made that part up."

"*Haaah.* It almost feels like I'm trying to squeeze useful information out of the president of an international conglomerate or a member of the nobility when I'm talking with you, Kousuke," Marino replied before taking another sip of her coffee.

"Did you need to go that far? It's beyond excessive. And hard to believe given the official explanation. That's what got me thinking that there must be another explanation for the transfer, too."

Indeed, I thought that Marino must have known what I knew.

But that was where my question lay. How did she know? It was something neither Yuika herself nor her stepbrother Iori had the slightest clue about. A truth that played a hugely important role in the game, too.

The same thing had happened with Nanami, too.

Although Nanami's status as a dungeon maid meant there were limits to what she could talk about, Marino would often chat with her for some reason. That was all the more reason why I felt Marino knew something, and why I assumed she had some other mysterious role to play.

I had questions about that angel, too. I had a hard time believing a woman in Marino's position would be in the dark about Nanami. And the fact that Marino had continued to provide Nanami a place to engage in activities of her own meant Marino must've known the whole story.

There was no end to my questions. So this time, I asked her directly.

I had accomplished one astounding feat after another already, without worrying about what Marino may think of me. It was way too late in the game for me to be concerned about that now.

"You found out that Yuika was being threatened by a 'weird' stalker and quickly called for her to come here."

That might have been to protect Yuika, or to use the girl for her own ends.

"You know, don't you, Marino?"

I was thankful that she'd transferred Yuika here. Both Iori and I were there for her at Tsukuyomi, after all.

That was also why I had been able to protect Yuika from the nefarious actor who was trying to use her blood this time.

"Yuika Hijiri is the Founding Saint's blood relative."

Marino didn't say anything.
She simply looked back at me with the same smile she always wore.
So that must have been her answer, then.

Chapter 12: Thus Was the Eroge Protagonist

It was already time for us to change our uniforms for the season.

The breeze was warm, the sun's rays were hot, and the people in the streets had started dressing lighter.

I wasn't feeling the heat myself thanks to the ice enhancement I'd placed on my stole, but Orange would remove his jacket entirely, while some other students fanned themselves with their hands.

"All of the petals have fallen and gone for the year, huh." I sighed, looking down the road that stretched out in front of me.

The once beautifully blooming row of cherry blossom trees, as if finished with their seasonal uniform swap early, had all been dyed a calm and mild light green.

The cherry blossom road had looked stunning when it had been all vibrant pinks and dancing petals, but with the season over, there was a different kind of charm to its now simple beauty.

How elegant it would have been to lean up against one of the trees and take in the view. Unfortunately, my promised meetup time was fast approaching.

I glanced around me, but there was no one in the vicinity.

Morning classes had started for the day, so this wasn't a surprise. But we'd scheduled the meetup for now, after the start of class. There was already someone waiting for me at the appointed spot.

He had short dark hair and a face that was neither hot nor ugly—exceedingly average, if not a bit cute. Even now in the warmer weather, he was wearing his entire school uniform, and he held the school's recommended bag in his hand.

Like before, he was looking at the shuttered school gate, but he didn't seem to be in any quandary about it this time.

"Aww, shoot, it's closed," I theatrically commented, coming up to him and staring at the gate. Then I turned to face the protagonist.

"'Sup, Iori."

"Good morning, Kousuke," Iori replied with a smile.

"Getting hotter and hotter every day, huh?"

"Yeah. A few days ago Rina, Class Rep, Orange, and I all went to get ice cream together."

"Rina, huh?" I said with a grin, prompting a weak smile from Iori.

"She told me that she wasn't going to let me get the best of her. That's when she told me to call her by her first name instead."

He'd gotten that rival recognition from Katorina. That was a sign he was making good progress. Getting permission to use her first name meant that she had acknowledged Iori's strength.

"But Rina said she didn't want to lose to you, either, Kousuke. She also admitted that there was a gap in strength between you two. And, well......"

Although he sighed a little, Iori didn't continue the thought any further.

"Anyway, sorry for dragging you out here at this odd time today."

"Ah, it's no big deal, I don't mind. Yuika sent me a message asking why I was skipping class, though. She seemed kinda angry."

Even though I was *always* cutting class.

Iori forced a smile with an exaggerated shrug.

"That's what I wanted to talk to you about today," he said before vigorously lowering his head. "Thank you."

"I don't feel like I've done much. Don't worry about it."

"Sure, maybe, but still, thank you... Did you hear about Yuika's past at all?"

I hadn't, actually, but I still knew all about it.

"Nah, I'm in the dark about it... Oh yeah, let me change the subject for a sec. There's something I want to ask you."

If this topic was going to come up, it'd be better if I heard it from her directly. There was a chance Yuika didn't want anyone to know. With that in mind, I changed the subject.

"What is it?"

"So, tell me, you're the type who'll send a happy birthday message to someone right at midnight, right?"

Iori was probably a bit of a romantic. The kind of guy who really

Chapter 12: Thus Was the Eroge Protagonist

valued anniversaries and birthdays and stuff. Otherwise, he wouldn't have gone out of his way to call me out here, at this precise time of day.

"I guess so. I usually wait for the perfect timing to send it out."

Iori chuckled. That was why it was completely obvious to me that this had something to do with that fateful day of ours.

"Out in front of the school, after classes have started. The closed school gate. You and me."

That was when we'd first met. We'd both gone about our business for several weeks after that.

And look what had happened to us in just a short while.

"A whole lot's happened to me since I took that first step with you."

"Just as much has happened with me, too."

The one thing I could say for sure was our days since had been a whirlwind, and we had both grown from it, each experiencing our share of successes and failures, too.

"Actually, when I first saw you, I was really surprised."

"'What the hell's with this guy and his huge scarf,' right?"

"*Hee-hee.* Sure, that too, but not exactly."

"Hmm, then were you shocked when we jumped over the gate and got chewed out for it?"

Iori happily chuckled.

"Oh, right, that did happen, huh? Sure, that was a surprise, too, but that wasn't what I meant, either. You've sorta guessed it already, right?"

Of course. With everything lined up like this, I could tell.

"When I was still a kid, I was involved in a little……no, actually, it was this incident big enough to end up on the news, and I had to be rescued."

Iori gazed up at the sky, seemingly reminiscing about a fond memory.

"The person who saved me back then? I thought they were really awesome. I wanted to be like them, too, since I wasn't able to protect my family at the time."

Iori was talking about Yuika's past. But I had denied knowing anything about it, which must have explained why he was being so vague. Iori turned his face down from the sky.

"But just thinking something can only get you so far."

"Right, only so far…"

Perhaps he was remembering what happened to Yuika. Or maybe he was recalling being attacked by that demon. He dropped his eyes and clenched his fist with gritted teeth.

"Exactly. No matter how much I want to save someone, or how much I try to make something happen, if I don't have the knowledge or strength to back it up, nothing will come of it."

Iori slowly opened his hands back up.

"That was the moment that made me want to be able to protect everyone if something ever happens."

Hearing Iori say this, I suddenly remembered something that had been on my mind—the fact that everyone had vastly changed from their in-game version. I had already noticed it here and there before.

From my perspective, this world was a game made into reality. However, each individual in this world had their own thoughts and personalities.

While their personalities may have largely been the same as their game counterparts', it went without saying that the people in this world were not game characters, but living, breathing individuals.

Everything wasn't guaranteed to be the same as it had been in the game, and all the characters would grow. They might end up weaker, but there was every chance they could end up tougher, too. Iori was getting stronger. Not only physically, either. He was also toughening up his mind.

"Kousuke, President Monica straight-up told me to join the Student Council."

It was a matter of course that Iori had caught President Monica's eye. To the point, I thought to myself it was about time.

"I couldn't give her an immediate answer, though."

"Why not?"

"I mean, I thought to myself, if I joined at my current level, would I really able to put in the work that the other members were putting in?"

"You totally can. Right from the get-go, too, I bet."

"President Monica told me the same thing. She also said this to me—"

Iori sighed quietly.

"'Don't you want to be like Kousuke Takioto? Or better, don't you want to *surpass* Kousuke Takioto?'"

"...Jeez, what the heck..."

"Hee-hee. She told me that the Student Council's the perfect place to get stronger. She said a lot of other stuff like that, too, and it helped me imagine the type of person I want to become."

"The type of person you wanna become, huh?"

"Yeah. Someone who's really awesome, strong, kind, and who saves everyone in need. So I'm joining the Student Council to get closer to that goal."

He closed his eyes and breathed in deep. Then, slowly exhaling, he opened them again.

Had something happened to Iori? I could make some simple guesses, but they were just that, and not necessarily correct. I might learn about it later down the line. If I asked, he might have simply told me.

"*Hah-hah, hah-hah-hah-hah*…… The Student Council, eh? Feels like a perfect fit for you. Guess I gotta kick myself into gear."

"Yeah, you better be ready. I'm going to keep moving forward. Straight on up. I've got the thirtieth layer of the Tsukuyomi Academy Dungeon in my sights."

There was a strong conviction in his eyes and a powerful vigor in the mana flowing from his body.

Aha, he'd probably entered what was known in *Magical ★Explorer* as his first "growth phase."

In that portion of the game, his base abilities increase, and he learns new skills, starts getting a good item collection together, and gains the ability to challenge a variety of different dungeons—in other words, all the conditions to ensure a drastic amount of growth line up at once.

It was coming. The explosive first stage of his development.

"Do you know why I called you out here, Kousuke?"

I made a show of shrugging my shoulders at his question.

"I wonder, seeing that classes've started and all…"

"I'm sorry about that, but you weren't going to show up anyway, right?"

We both shared a laugh. Since when had he started talking back to me like this?

"Of course I know the reason you called me out here."

Making sure to have us meet while morning classes were going on. The school gate, with no one else around. He had found his resolve, just like me.

"That road ain't gonna be an easy one, now. Someone else is fighting down that same path, using any method at their disposal to get there."

I definitely didn't need to tell you who exactly that was, now did I, Iori?

"Yeah. I get that. But I still wanted to say it out loud."

I could guess what Iori was about to say. He was trying to replicate that day. He was going to accept my challenge.

So how was I supposed to respond? Actually, that was a given.

He turned his eyes toward the school building.

"Not much time's passed since I came to this academy, but I'm seriously glad I came."

Was he thinking back to something? He looked up to the sky and sighed.

As Iori had progressed through different events and the story at large, he hadn't just strengthened his abilities, but also his heart as well. He wasn't the usual Iori. Not the somewhat unreliable, sort of adorable puppy dog–like Iori. Yet the Iori in front of me was the Iori I knew. I had seen him over and over and over again in-game.

He was the Iori Hijiri who would face down any boss, no matter how difficult, for the sake of the game's heroines.

"This place has fantastic facilities for getting stronger. Empathetic teachers," he said, slowly considering his words as he spoke.

"Plenty of amazing friends you can rely on. Not to mention the dungeons, the best possible stage to test for how strong you've become. And more than anything…"

Iori paused and stared at me.

"It has people to aspire to. Rivals."

I needed to respond to his feelings. I sent mana into my stole, then I scattered the mana that still overflowed from me all around, as much as my enormous reserves would allow.

Finally, I cast a smirk down on Iori. Even as he looked back up at me, his expression never faltered.

"Kousuke. I'm going to clear the fortieth floor soon. I don't really know why, but I feel like I'll be able to do it easily."

His eyes were filled with such conviction I couldn't look away.

"Yeah, you're gonna get stronger. That's my prediction for you. You've got a tremendous, unimaginable power slumbering inside you."

"This time, I'm going to be the one to make a declaration here."

This was my cue for a bold smile. I had no plans on losing to him, after all.

"The strongest student at Tsukuyomi Magic Academy…is going to be me, Iori Hijiri!"

Afterword

Good day. Irisu the radio silent. I'm still alive, I promise.

—Acknowledgments—

To Kannatuki. Thank you very much. All jokes aside, I am always grateful for your work. The illustrations were as wonderful as always. Ivy, Miss Sakura, Gabby, and Orange. Phenomenal, all of them! With Gabby, I felt like I could hear her high-pitched laughter in my head just looking at the rough sketch. (How I wish I could hear her call me big brother.)

To Yukari Higa, thank you as always. I'm grateful for your painstaking attention to detail, not only in the depictions of the characters, but in the backgrounds as well, along with the various references and jokes you playfully sprinkle in. And above all else, the sexiness. Everything is absolutely fantastic.

If any of my readers have yet to see the manga adaptation, I would highly recommend you check it out. It's superb quality.

Also, I'd like to bring your attention not just to the main characters, but to the background characters, too! They're all cute enough to steal the leading role for themselves! The manga is currently being serialized in *Young Ace Up*, so definitely take a look.

The first volume of the manga adaptation is right on the horizon as well, so I ask you to support the series there, too. I mentioned this in the announcement as well, but it comes with quite an extravagant extra bonus!

To Mikeou. Thank you very much for your *extremely* cute-yet-erotic Yuika!

Just seeing the illustration you provided sent my fantasies into overdrive......! Oh, how I'd love to be woken up in the morning by a little sister like her. I wouldn't have any time to waste on going to school, that's for sure.

To my capable editor Miyakawa. I am sorry for always, consistently, and endlessly putting you through so much trouble. I'm only able to continue writing because of all your hard work. If you weren't here, this story definitely wouldn't have made it anywhere close to volume four. Thank you so very much.

—Announcements—

The first volume of the *Magical★Explorer* manga adaptation will go on sale starting March 10, 2021.

As for the special bonus, a super famous voice actress has lent her voice to Ludie, to provide a wonderful extra for everyone who purchases the volume. Please check Twitter for the details!

The official Twitter account is at https://twitter.com/Majieku_ (@majieku_).

I hope you'll pick it up!

—Idle Chitchat, Etc.—

Do you know *Dragon **st V*? It's a very famous game, so I imagine even those who haven't played it have heard of it. It even got made into a movie.

In this game there's a wedding event, and you can progress through the story with the person you marry. You can marry two of the heroines (with a third option being added in the remake). This gave rise to a large controversy among the fans.

You can marry your childhood friend Bi**nca or the rich girl N*ra (after marrying, you get bonus money and armor). I imagine some of you out there were really torn over who to marry during your first playthrough. I wasn't even given the luxury.

I received a divine message from a god I absolutely couldn't defy.

Big Sister: "I'm marrying Bi**nca, so you marry N*ra, got it?"

▶ Afterword

Me: "............... (I was speechless)"
I had to choose N*ra.
To be honest, I would have preferred the childhood friend, Bi**nca. After all, she was a beautiful older sister figure, and she and the hero had adventured in a haunted castle when they were young. I was attached to her, and I had a bit of a crush on her even as a young child. But I couldn't possibly defy my sister, could I?
Now allow me to confess something here.
After getting married, I hated it just as much as I thought I would, at first. Why did I have to marry someone like N*ra? Why did I have to go through this aristocratic wedding nonsense? Et cetera, et cetera. As such, I'm sure N*ra hated it just as much. She probably thought to herself, *Am I really going to go on some adventure with a crappy dude who doesn't care about me at all?*
However, N*ra still says thoughtful, considerate things to Bi**nca before the wedding! She joins the protagonist, dressed in a grungy turban and cloak and little better than a wandering vagabond, on a grand adventure, and offers up her life to him! She's a fantastic wife who is always concerned for your well-being.
I had a change of heart. I felt awful about how I had treated this girl who supported me so admirably. One of the biggest mistakes of my life. Incidentally, this ended up being one of the reasons your humble Irisu here fell in love with rich-girl characters. Basically, it's all my big sister's fault. I hope you're all looking forward to seeing more of rich-girl Gabby in the next volume.
Those in the Bi**nca camp all scream that we N*ra fans are simply all about the money, and that as knights, we should be ashamed. Actually, my sister also mentioned the money stuff, assuring me that "You'll get money and strong armor for free, so it's a pretty good deal." Yeah, except I still wondered, *If it's such a good deal, why is she insisting on Bi**nca instead?* You'd never get me to say that out loud, though.
It was simply that money didn't dictate my choices. I'll admit that some people are of the opinion that money is what matters, and I can't deny that. It pains me to say that, in reality, money is a precious commodity. But even if she was broke, I'd still choose N*ra, her wonderful, fantastic—wait, shoot, I'm running out of spa